BRIGHT, BROKEN THINGS

A GOOD THINGS COME PREQUEL

LINDA SHANTZ

Bright, Broken Things

eBook edition ISBN: 978-1-990436-12-3

Paperback ISBN: 978-1-990436-11-6

ALSO BY LINDA SHANTZ

For updates and bonus chapters, sign up for Linda's newsletter at

https://www.lindashantz.com/writes

HELP WANTED:

Seeking experienced help for two positions on Thoroughbred breeding farm in King, Ontario.

General farm staff (Full-time, permanent). Position involves turnout/in, feeding, mucking and other general farm maintenance. Must be comfortable handling Thoroughbreds of all ages: mares and foals, yearlings and track layups. Six days a week, 7am-4pm with breaks and an hour for lunch. This is not a riding position. Must be reliable with own transportation. Accommodations may be available.

Part-time, temporary, afternoons, starting yearlings. Possibility of winter employment.

To apply, please email triplestripestables@ gmail.com

CHAPTER ONE

MINUTES, hours, days. They rushed past like the air outside his window — his arm outstretched, flat palm providing little resistance to the vehicle's speed. He half expected pieces to start flying off his rusty old Mustang, like parts of a spaceship's fuselage burning up in the atmosphere.

Fleeing the scene of the train wreck that had been his life had been easy. The beat-up car put miles between himself and his native Calgary readily enough, but the distance had done nothing to dilute his feelings. They clung to the roof of his dusty vehicle, cackling along to a soundtrack he had no one to blame for but himself. He'd picked the tunes, the Mustang vibrating with pounding bass, the lyrics keeping his torment a fresh, open wound.

The truth was, he had no one to blame but himself for any of it. Why had he stayed so long?

Because there was still hope, wasn't there? Until the minister said those words, there was still hope.

He'd stared at her profile from where he stood at the back of the church, willing her to look at him. But she didn't. She didn't waver in her conviction as she spoke the last part of the vows.

Till death do us part.

It felt dramatic. It felt like his own death.

He'd left his hangover behind somewhere around Winnipeg, chased away by caffeine and sleeplessness. Dropping into the US might have taken a few hours off his trip, but he wasn't exactly in a hurry to get where he was going — because he wasn't even sure he knew where that was. All that mattered was getting away, like a sore horse sprinting from pain. If you ran fast enough, you didn't feel it. Run now, think later.

Plus, he didn't have a passport. Did he need one? He hadn't bothered to check. But, crossing the border, he would've been tempted to stop in Chicago — he'd heard Arlington Park racetrack was nice — or to keep heading south. It would be easy to find a job working with horses in Kentucky.

But he had one remaining friend in this world — not counting his mom — and if ever he needed a friend, it was now. So he'd stick to the fragile remnants of his plan — a plan that had become instead an escape — and keep traveling east.

Manitoba gave way to Northern Ontario. Kenora, Thunder Bay, Sault-Ste Marie, Sudbury, the Trans-Canada Highway his constant companion. He really didn't see any of it, and a tiny part of him felt bad. He might never make such an epic journey across this great country again. But there was no room right now for appreciation; he was too consumed with flight.

He should have taken off on New Year's Day. But he'd remained, hoping she'd change her mind. Hoping she'd reverse her refusal and pick him. Hoping until there was no hope left.

And *what a beautiful wedding.*

It's what the people who didn't know the sordid story said. The ones that did looked at him with pity, whispering behind hands meant to muffle their words, as if they could spare him the torment.

Had they omitted that part about "speak now or forever hold your peace" because of him? Because they'd feared he'd stand up with some desperate last-minute plea and ruin everything?

Pick me. Love me. It was supposed to be him up there, gazing into her beautiful face, saying those words. Sealing it all with a kiss.

Part of him didn't want to hide from the pain. Didn't want to be rid of it. He wanted to feel it all, let it be part of him. Remember it — her — forever. And never, ever let himself be so taken again.

Diesel fumes overpowered his nostrils as he walked out of the ON Route rest stop somewhere north of Toronto, the country's largest metropolis. Humidity clung to his skin like his emotional baggage. His most recent Tim Horton's coffee burned his palm as he clutched it, a searing reminder his ability to feel pain was probably bottomless at this point. He was the guy who felt too much. It was exhausting.

The brew was probably higher octane than the gas he pumped into his ancient car and he'd consumed enough of it over the past few days — was it two or three? — to keep him awake for a week. Sitting behind the wheel again, the dusty bucket seat molding to his back, he had to at least be grateful for the fact the battered car had made it this far. One day, maybe, he'd restore it properly so it could be called vintage. But that would have to wait until he cared again.

Now he pressed his phone to his ear, listening to the ringing drone until a friendly chuckle interrupted it. "Miller. Thought I might be hearing from you. Where are you?"

"I don't know. Barrie?"

"You made good time. I'm not gonna ask how."

"Yeah. Don't."

"You're about an hour out. I'll text you the address. See you soon."

When the text came, he copied the address into Google Maps and let the GPS-lady voice tell him where to go, wishing the direction of the rest of his life was that easy. Driving south on the 400 highway toward Toronto, he started seeing signs for the big airport. Woodbine, Canada's largest racetrack, was over there somewhere, buried amid urban sprawl and industry, jets flying low above.

That's where he should head. It's where she'd said he belonged, back when they had plans. Plans he'd thought were theirs. Now, somehow, he had to reframe them as his alone.

The best thing he'd done when he'd rebuilt the old Mustang — only the most recent of one of its many lives — was sink his money into an aftermarket stereo, the memory of those days when his father and brothers had helped him now tainted with irony. It was the music that had gotten him through. He used it to manipulate his moods. When Three Days Grace and Cursive left him feeling too battered, he'd find some Switchfoot, though the California band could still pierce him with agonizing truth. Because this was indeed a beautiful letdown, and he had gloriously crashed and burned.

Will Callaghan greeted him like the old friend he was.

"I've gotta go to work. Don't wait up," Will apologized. "Make yourself at home."

Will probably thought he meant it, but having your morose buddy crash on your couch in your one-room apartment would get old pretty fast.

"Thanks," Nate said, setting a tired overnight bag, the original colour of which he'd long ago forgotten, just inside the door.

Will paused next to him. "You all right?"

His friend meant that too. It wasn't just a platitude; his compassion was genuine. But Nate clamped his teeth together and forced one corner of his mouth up, sending the deadness he felt to his eyes with a grimace. He couldn't answer, because he wasn't, not really. He didn't miss the concern in the look Will returned as his friend rested a hand on his shoulder and slipped into the hall.

Will's downtown Toronto loft was one big room in an old converted red brick factory building, though he'd curtained off a corner next to the bathroom for a bedroom area. Nate felt like Goldilocks, peering at the queen-sized bed, which looked far comfier than the couch. But Will worked late — said he'd be home at some ungodly hour — and it would definitely be bad to exploit his hospitality by stealing his bed. The couch was a step up from the back seat of his car, anyway.

He didn't shower; he didn't change, he just collapsed on the warped and worn sofa. Any doubts he'd had about being able to sleep after three days of too much coffee crumbled away the second his body hit the comfy cushions. Dragging the throw draped over the back of the couch onto himself — the loft was climate controlled, unlike the Mustang — he tucked into its length, resting his head on one of the mismatched pillows, his eyelids heavy.

He'd thought when he came to this city, it would be to conquer. There had been a plan. But when he left Calgary, the only plan was to get the hell out.

CHAPTER TWO

THE SAFEST PLACE in the world was on the back of a racehorse.

Some might beg to differ. Being five feet from the ground on an inherently unpredictable animal, with stirrup irons so short, her knees rested against the horse's withers — it might seem to others a dangerous place to be. For Liv, though, it was sanctuary.

She didn't know who'd said it first: *In riding a horse, we borrow freedom.* But borrowing it wasn't good enough. She wanted to capture it; devise a method of encapsulating it so it was forever at her disposal.

It was a barrier, or at the very least a buffer, from those around her; this powerful, vivacious creature her equalizer and shield. The connection she shared with the animal beneath her made up for what she failed to feel for the humans in her periphery. Behind goggles, under a helmet, her long dark hair tucked neatly beneath a navy kerchief, she could pretend she was invisible, or at least invincible. When someone did venture to talk to her, the horse was her translator, the common ground which let her feel a little less of an outcast, though she would never be one of them.

She called the filly in to the clocker. "Just Stellar, five-eighths." It was as much as she needed to say to anyone. Her horse's name and the distance. No more, no less.

"'Morning." A middle-aged exercise rider on a horse that was tall and dark bay and devoid of white markings greeted her as he materialized from the darkness of the tunnel, returning from the track as she headed for it.

She nodded and gave a slight smile, though she didn't manage to push words from her throat. With her dark goggles, he wouldn't know she wasn't making eye contact. Her gaze dropped instead to the neat line of his mount's mane, the slight lift of the dark bay's head before it dropped with each step. Each encounter was an assessment: how much to give? How much to trust? It kept others at a distance. That was how she wanted it. Call it self-protection.

Aluminum-shod hoofbeats on the rubber bricks underfoot echoed with the voices of exercise riders coming and going, bouncing off the cool concrete walls of the passage beneath the expansive turf course that surrounded the main synthetic surface. Her nostrils filled with leather and manure, warm horses and humans, the mingling smells trapped in the damp space.

Just Stellar followed the horses in front of her, up to the track. Glancing left to be sure no one was coming out of the chute, Liv negotiated traffic, finding her own space on the outside rail to back up — jogging clockwise toward the tall white finishing post across from the grandstand, staying clear of the gallopers going the opposite direction in the middle of the track.

Once she was out here — pausing at the wire to face the infield, Just Stellar standing until Liv gave the okay to join the flow of gallopers, together but separate — nothing else mattered. Not school, not the people around her, not a list of names applying for the job she'd posted for her father's farm. With the air rushing past her ears, carrying her mount's mane, the only sounds that registered were the thrum of hooves on the Tapeta surface and the steady rhythm of the filly's breathing, cycling in time with her own heart. This was where she belonged. The only place she felt truly herself.

Like a jet taking off at the nearby international airport, when they reached the backstretch she checked the flight path was clear and dropped the filly to the rail, crouching low so they were up to speed when they reached the five-eighths pole and the clocker started timing. In front of her, Just Stellar's long neck pulsed faster, ears laced back, black mane whipping. The filly skirted the turn, legs like pistons firing, the oxygen sucked into her lungs through flared nostrils feeding each stride and the stretch opened in front of them, wide and welcoming and all theirs. At that moment, there was nothing else. No gallopers, no looming empty grandstand, no landscaped infield and massive tote board. Just real estate to be conquered, a stop-watch to record a number — a number that could never capture the feeling of being one with such a remarkable creature, one that almost allowed her science-filled head to think such an animal had to have been created by something caring and intelligent. This was no random freak of nature.

If only the feeling wasn't so temporary, so fleeting. All the more reason to cherish it. She should be satisfied she got to play a part. Happy she got to come here in the summer, and some weekends once she was back at school, to share, in some small way, their lives. But she wanted more. Was that selfish?

It felt wrong. So many twenty-two-year-old women would covet her life. Living on a beautiful farm in the heart of King Township's Thoroughbred horse country, about to enter her third year at the prestigious Ontario Veterinary College, her future secure. She'd endured her share of sly talk at school about her connections getting her admitted to the program, because grades alone didn't get you in. And there was some truth to that, because maybe those connections had helped smooth over the social deficits revealed during the interview process. It made her feel as if it was all a ruse, like she'd fooled everyone somehow.

Up here, she didn't have to pretend. This, here, was the real her. The one who would soon be back in OVC's lecture halls was an imposter. And it wasn't that she hated school, it was just that it felt like a performance. Acting had never been her forté. *Note to self: get better.*

"Hey, Liv. When are you going to get your license?"

She snapped her head toward the voice, relieved when she connected it to Dhruv Patel. Dhruv was an unlikely representation of a jock's agent. He was tall and handsome, always well-dressed — and happily married with three teenage sons. Dhruv didn't try to flirt. She never heard Dhruv making off-colour comments about anyone. He was completely professional. She liked him. He was trustworthy.

And he meant her apprentice jockey license, of course. Her smile came easily for him as Just Stellar sauntered past. "You'll be the first to know."

The smile lingered as she headed back to the barn, both her and the horse sated, for now. But it soon faded, because this was when they all raged: the voices in her head that told her she didn't want to be a vet.

This is what she wanted. To get her license. To ride.

But it was just a dream. That was all. It wasn't as if she was entitled to it. Summer was almost over, and soon she'd pack the dream back up and tuck it away where it belonged.

CHAPTER THREE

So here he was. Happy birthday to him, waking up on the couch of the only person he knew in a strange metropolitan city — with no prospects.

He folded the throw he'd covered himself with and went to the kitchen, stomach rumbling. He couldn't remember when he'd properly eaten last. In his sleep of the dead, he hadn't heard Will come home, but there was evidence in the refrigerator: a couple of takeout containers. There were advantages to working in a restaurant. Will probably never went hungry.

One had two big chunks of cooked salmon; the other roasted potatoes. He opted for the potatoes, throwing them in the microwave. Grabbing a beer as he waited, he checked the drawers until he found the cutlery. With the steaming container in one hand and bottle in the other, he returned to the couch. Looked like a fine breakfast.

"Find something to eat?"

He twisted from where he sprawled on the couch, nursing his beer, to find Will squinting under furrowed brows. Not an angry look, just obviously not awake.

"Yeah, thanks." Then he raised the bottle. "I was actually sober for three days. Admirable while it lasted."

Will chuckled and disappeared into the bathroom. When he emerged, he went to the kitchen and started a pot of coffee. As much as Nate admitted that would have been a wiser choice than the Molson Canadian in his hand, he couldn't stomach the thought of any more coffee yet.

Will sank into an adjacent chair with a mug. "We should go out tonight. Celebrate."

Nate swung his legs off the couch, feeling a twinge of guilt that he was probably in Will's favourite spot, facing the television. "What are we celebrating, exactly?" He couldn't find a decent reason himself.

"Your arrival? Your birthday?"

He tried to muster a grin, but it was a little weak. "You remember that, eh?"

"C'mon, you're my oldest friend. How could I forget?"

Maybe because they hadn't seen much of each other in four years, since Will had come to Toronto to go to school on a music scholarship. They'd stayed in touch, and made sure they saw each other when Will came home at Christmas, but it wasn't the same. Was it ever?

He didn't realize till now how much he'd missed Will. He didn't really feel like going out, but couldn't ignore the gesture. "Don't you have to work?" he asked.

Will waved a hand. "I took the time off."

Nate looked at him sideways, reading between the lines. *My buddy just arrived in town and I think he might self-destruct, so he needs me more than you do.*

"All right. As long as you're buying, because I'm pretty much broke. Show me the town."

Or a snapshot of it, as it turned out. He would have much preferred to spend the evening the way they'd passed the afternoon: kicking around Will's loft, playing a bit of music. Eating a proper meal — thanks, again, to Will. Instead, the small club they ended up at was packed with bodies, most of them drunk, creating heat the air conditioning couldn't keep up with as they writhed to music. It was dark, and the sound was bad, and the only way to deal with it was to accept the beer Will bought him.

"Welcome to Toronto," his friend shouted over the din.

Nate clinked the long neck of his bottle to Will's with another unconvincing smile.

He didn't say no when someone asked him to dance, allowing himself to be pulled to the floor, the two of them making their own space amid the crush. It wasn't long before she was all over him, her too-heavy perfume invading his nostrils as her hands raked his hair, lips on his ear. It only made him feel worse. Why was he even here? This wouldn't fill the empty, it would just bottom him out more.

"You're cute," she whisper-yelled, the pitch of her voice piercing his already-aggravated eardrums. He could feel her breath, drenched with cheap beer. *Lovely.* He wasn't sure he could say the same thing about her at the moment, though it wasn't fair to pass judgment in her current state of inebriation.

I get that a lot, he almost responded. It was the height thing. So he was short. She didn't seem to mind so much. These Toronto girls were bold.

The tempo slowed, and he detached himself from her like he was pulling a tick off one of his dad's Golden Retrievers. Bloodthirsty things. "I've gotta —" He thumbed over his shoulder, hoping it might be in the general direction of the restrooms. Not that she probably knew where they were, either. Or maybe she did. Maybe she was a regular.

She fluttered the fingers of one hand at him. "Hurry back!"

Yeah... maybe not.

He weaved through sweaty bodies, his running shoes sticking to the tacky floor. Someone tripped and spilled beer on his shirt. *Great.* At least he'd smell like he'd had a good time. Where the hell was Will?

Finally, he spotted his friend, who did look as if he was enjoying himself. Nate pulled out his phone and sent Will a text, resisting the temptation to write SOS. *I'm getting out of here.*

He waited by the bar for a few moments, just in case Will wanted to leave, too. Watched his friend react to his phone, read the screen, scan the room, settle on Nate. Nate waved. Will gave him a thumbs-up, typed something back, and kept dancing.

The buzz of Will's message came. *You sure you're okay?*

Nate responded. *Yeah. I'll be fine. Enjoy yourself.*

So much for his oldest friend taking care of him. But he didn't really need Will to take care of him. Didn't want it. As he found the exit, Talking Heads' "Once In A Lifetime" started up. It seemed à propos. *This is not my beautiful anything.*

Outside, he breathed the city air, full of exhaust fumes and a fishiness from nearby Lake Ontario. Someone in the vicinity was smoking pot; he caught a whiff of the skunky scent. Would that make him happy? Or pretend-happy? Not likely.

Time to investigate public transit. He could figure out how to get back to Will's. It wasn't that far, but far enough he didn't want to walk it. He didn't know how long it was going to take to find a job, so he'd better budget his cash, which ruled out a taxi or Uber.

So, the TTC: Toronto transit. They must have a website.

He took full advantage of looking under nineteen to get a youth fare; it saved him almost a buck. He wasn't going to bring it to anyone's attention that he was, as of today, twenty-three.

Of course he'd had to show his ID at the club, but no one had asked here.

There was hardly anyone on the train, so finding a seat wasn't an issue. The only one who made eye contact with him was the German Shepherd sitting with a forty-ish looking woman on the other side. The dog grinned at him. Nate smiled back, then stared at his phone like everyone else.

At Will's loft, he kicked off his shoes and grabbed a Canadian from the fridge, but promised himself he wouldn't be that guy in Lowest of the Low's "Eternal Fatalist," parking himself on his buddy's couch and drinking all his beer. He had to find a job.

He should just go to the racetrack, though spring would have been a better time of year for that, when everyone was looking. Al, the trainer he'd worked for back home, had given him a couple of numbers, suggesting he could gallop in the mornings and start yearlings in the afternoons. He wouldn't be going in completely on a whim.

But at the track, he would stand out. He'd be pigeon-holed, with his size. Why else would a guy like him come east? A year ago, he'd been that guy. The guy who would be exactly that — eager to become a rider. The guy who thought he had it all. He'd given up on that guy.

He thumbed through a job site. Maybe he should work in a factory. Not do horses at all. Defy the stereotype his body had decided he was best suited for. Find a schedule complimentary to Will's. Be anonymous. He could just be a lackey with a job that paid the bills and got together with his buddy to play some music. Forever sixteen. It would be like old times.

Going back to school wasn't really an option. He'd lost his free pass, dropping out and leaving his home province. Invoked his father's fury when he'd given up. All that tuition money down the drain. He was already a disappointment. He wasn't super-smart, like his older brother Phil, the lawyer. Or tall, like his younger brother Tim, on his way to a career as a professional hockey player. His father had held fast to that dream for Nate too, until he'd stopped growing. It was like Reid Miller took it as a personal insult. At least his mother loved him, no matter what.

He kept flipping. Production jobs. Restaurant grunt jobs that wouldn't pay enough to survive. He might eat okay, but sure wouldn't be able to afford an apartment in this city. Then he saw it. A horse job. It stood out like a beacon of hope, the first time he'd felt any since his had been crushed on New Year's Eve at exactly eleven fifty-five.

He was drunk — again — but it didn't matter. He knew enough not to drunk-text his ex two days into her honeymoon. But a drunk job application? He was sure he wouldn't regret that in the morning. This job was written for him. It could be the thing that would turn his life around.

It wasn't hard to piece together a resumé; the website made it easy to plug in job experience and education. He had to look up how to do a cover letter, though. Was it overkill? He didn't care. This was his lifeline.

He hit send.

CHAPTER FOUR

SHE HADN'T MEANT to get attached. There was no helping it, though.

It wasn't that the filly was pretty, with her delicate head, still very much a baby face at eighteen months. It wasn't that she was flashy, liberally decorated with white bling from the wide, crooked blaze that dipped into one nostril to the high stockings on three of her legs. It wasn't even the balance of her conformation, the lovely shape of her feet, the richness of her bay coat, more gold than red. It was the way she soaked up the affection Liv all too willingly dispensed, thirsty like a sponge that had dried in the sun.

Claire was the smallest of the yearlings, but very much in charge of her little group of friends. A benevolent dictator, who only needed to shift her head, giving her pasture mates a glimpse of one of her wall eyes to command respect. Liv gave her the same respect.

She blew softly into the filly's nostril, pink and flared. Claire blew back, and Liv smiled as she snapped on the rope lead. Gone, gone, gone. Her heart was gone to this one.

Guiding Claire through the gate and re-latching it, they left the other fillies clambering against the steel barrier, trying to figure out who was boss now that their leader had left.

The barn was dark and free of humans now that the horses were fed and the staff had gone home. Liv left Claire to the hay piled in the corner of the stall while she went to the tack room to gather what she needed.

The filly was smart, too, standing on the wall attached to the thick rubber bungee, as quiet as a seasoned racehorse. Liv groomed her quickly, then positioned the exercise saddle and pads, Claire's only response a swivel of her ear. She slipped the bit into the filly's mouth, and slid the headstall over the small, flexible ears. Then she rigged up the long driving lines, securing them to the saddle on either side, and led Claire to the sand ring outside the barn.

She didn't have the most demonstrative relationship with her father, but she loved him for the soft spot that had nudged him to bid on a sorry little weanling in the Keeneland sales ring. Scrawny and rough-coated, the bay filly had stood out for all the wrong reasons, but Claude Lachance had seen the diamond in the rough.

When Claire had walked off the transport from Kentucky, farm manager Geai Doucet, always quick to inspire names, commented she looked like a chocolate eclair with her blaze bisecting the golden bay of her face, topped with a wispy black forelock — and someone needed to feed her a dozen or so to fatten her up. So Claire she'd become, and to Liv, she was sweeter than an entire tray of decadent pastries. She'd latched onto the filly like a baby duckling, when it should have been the other way around. Now, after months of careful nurturing, her training had begun.

Ground driving was like a dance, Liv guiding the filly first in a circle around her at the end of the lines, then sweeping behind like she was water skiing, slipping over the wake to direct Claire the other way. She felt the filly mouthing the bit, accepting it if not reaching for it, moving forward from the pressure of the lines on her sides that in time would be replaced by legs. Liv imagined she was pushing air through a bellows as they maneuvered around the ring. Slow and steady, changing direction across the diagonal, every so often halting as Liv coordinated her long, low, *hoooo* with consistent pressure on the lines, though it was more that she removed her encouragement that stopped Claire's forward momentum.

She caught sight of the stocky figure leaning on the top rail out of the corner of her eye and grinned.

"She looks good!" Geai called to her in French.

"Open the gate!"

He didn't move. "You sure?"

"Yes, I'm sure." Claire might only be a yearling, but she already trusted this filly more than anyone — save for Geai — in her life.

Geai nodded, not looking particularly concerned, and opened the gate. When it came down to it, he trusted her judgment. She steered Claire toward the gap, funneling the little filly through.

"Such a brave girl," she crooned.

Claire's head rose slightly, ears pricked as she filtered new information. It wasn't as if the surroundings were unfamiliar — she'd made the walk from the yearling fillies' paddock to the barn every day since last winter. The context was different, however, and horses typically viewed novel situations with suspicion. Claire, however, tackled each fresh experience with confidence Liv both admired and envied. Was it weird to take life lessons from a year-old Thoroughbred? She wanted to follow the filly wherever she went.

She kept the adventure short, not wanting to test her luck,

directing Claire back into the enclosure. Geai, who had watched the whole thing, went to the filly's head, holding her while Liv collected the lines again.

"She's ready for the next step," Liv said, taking advantage of Geai's assistance to remove the off side line, neatly tying it up. She undid the twine under Claire's girth that connected the stirrups to keep them secure, then ran up the irons. "It's only two weeks till the rest of them start. She can start early."

"So you can do it." Geai's grin was wry.

"Of course." She smiled coyly back.

"We still need to hire someone."

"For the rest of them, yes," she admitted. She wished she could do them all herself, but it would be impossible with her course load this fall.

"How are you going to continue with Claire once you're back at school?"

"I'll make it work." One way or another. Claire was the main reason she insisted on living at home when the university was over an hour away.

"Let's back her today," she said, letting thoughts of needing someone else to start yearlings fade into things she'd worry about later. She cast a sideways glance at Geai. "You're not going to give me a hard time about this?"

"Back in the day, we always used to start them in August," he said in his best sage old man voice. "They're babied these days."

"Horses were sounder then, though," Liv insisted.

"Were they? Or did the way we trained them make them that way?"

He had a point. But didn't North America's need for speed and oversized sale yearlings contribute to the breed's decline? There were too many variables to know. If inbreeding were to blame for today's perceived unsoundness, then Claire should be injury-free if they trained her right. Her obscure New York-bred pedigree was a complete outcross, though she had a dash of Northern Dancer blood. Maybe that's where all her splashy white came from.

"Hold her?" Liv asked. "I'll grab my helmet."

She retrieved it from the passenger seat of her nondescript Nissan hatchback, the car black somewhere under an even film of dust. Her kerchief was still damp from galloping that morning at the racetrack and felt gross as she slid it over her dark hair and pressed on the helmet. The sensation would pass. One day she'd learn to keep a few clean, dry extras stashed in the vehicle.

Geai waited with Claire in the stall and Liv exchanged the long line he held for the rope lead she'd used earlier, snapping it to the leather halter Claire wore under her bridle. Liv deposited the line in the barn's aisle and slid the door shut behind her.

She didn't need words here. Her grandfather had taught her to ride, but Geai had taught her to gallop and start babies. If she was going to ride horses that weren't hers, this made her happier than drilling sales ponies and horses under Daniel Lachance's strict tutelage.

One hand resting on the filly's withers, one on the seat of the saddle, she bent her left leg, Geai grasping her ankle and giving her a boost. Liv braced against it, springing high enough to straighten her arms, allowing Claire to feel some weight, observing the filly's reaction as she did so. A flick of her ears, a shift of her legs to rebalance — that was all. Liv let herself drop back to the straw, and the next time Geai lifted, she leaned, then draped her torso over the tack — they called it bellying for obvious reasons.

Claire turned her head, and Liv grinned at her. "Hey there, little miss. What do you think?" Then she reached out and touched a finger to the soft pink between the filly's nostrils. "Go ahead and walk her, Geai."

The lurch as the farm manager turned Claire within the confines of the stall felt awkward with her body draped across the tack like this, and Liv was aware how close her head was to the walls, but Geai was the most reliable ground person she could ever want. He'd take care of her.

The movement stopped, and she relaxed for a moment. "I'm throwing my leg over, Geai."

He got a warning for that. She wouldn't always take this step on the first day, but Claire was being a gem. Liv pushed on her palms so she was upright again, arms straight, and checked in with Claire, letting the filly adjust to the weight shift. *You good? Good.* Then she scissored her right leg over and gradually transferred her weight from her arms to ease herself into the saddle. Maybe if she hadn't been into horses, she would have taken more of an interest in gymnastics.

"What a good girl," she murmured, reaching down to stroke Claire's neck, first on one side, then the other. Then she dismounted, landing neatly back on the straw. She looked at Geai. "Once more? Right up this time."

He nodded. A little more lift, a little more spring, and she was astride. Rock star Claire didn't bat an eye.

"That's good for today," she said when she was on the ground again. She took the lead from Geai. "Thank you."

"Always my pleasure," he said.

Liv slipped off the headstall and snapped the wall tie to Claire's halter. "We'll be outside before you know it."

Geai followed her as she took the equipment to the tack room. "Are you ready to start interviewing?"

Liv met his eyes, the unspoken communicated. Hiring had always been Geai's job, but one day running the farm would become her responsibility and he and her father had decided this task would be a good one for her to take on — because talking to strangers wasn't exactly her strength. Geai didn't believe in coddling weakness.

They needed a general farm worker in addition to an exercise rider, so she'd posted positions for both. There were a surprising number of applicants so far, though many of them were obvious nos — kids who had watched too much *Heartland* and decided they were horse whisperers, claiming to have been riding since they were two. Some applicants for the farm job were older, from unlikely backgrounds — no equine experience per se, but looking for a lifestyle change. They weren't immediate discounts but required more discernment. She'd have to weed them out, deciding who to invite for interviews. She could do this. At least they'd be talking about horses.

"Same time tomorrow?" she asked Geai, and he nodded, leaving her to the tack.

She scanned her email, noticing more applicants. She needed to tackle this before it got overwhelming. Time was ticking away, school approaching much too quickly. After turning Claire back out and putting away the equipment, she drove her car to the smaller stable that housed the farm office.

It was easier to filter through the job responses on the computer than on her phone. *Good experience, Liv.* For her future at the farm. For her future as a veterinarian. Maybe for life in general. Of course, if she were better adjusted, she'd know more of the exercise riders at Woodbine. She'd chat with them, coming and going from the track. She'd have friends, someone who would be interested in starting the yearlings this year.

Friends or no friends — it was most definitely closer to the latter for her — she should have asked around more. But recruiting wasn't her strength either. It would have attracted unwanted attention. Instead, she'd sent a casting call out into the universe.

She stopped, the application she'd just opened catching her eye.

Perhaps the universe had sent a prospect back. She must be misunderstanding the cover letter, because it suggested this one was interested in both jobs. How great would it be to take care of what they needed in one fell swoop? The only problem was that the applicant was male, and probably her age, she deduced from his education. But the whole point of her hiring someone was because she wouldn't be around to do it herself, so what did it matter?

CHAPTER FIVE

HE GOT up when he woke up — around daybreak — the fog clearing from his not-quite hungover brain. Wait — had he texted his ex last night? No. Thank goodness. He should really take her number out of his phone to safeguard against such stupidity.

But — a job, that was it. In his dreams, he'd found himself on some nightmare farm with broken fences and feral yearlings and thoughts like, *what if I die here?* Would anyone but his mother care? There had been no name on the posting, so he had no way of checking the place out. But the location was King City, which was a pretty posh area from what he understood. He flipped through his email, but there was no response. Of course it was too soon. He wasn't impressive enough to leave a farm manager falling over themselves to speak to him. The nightmare farm was probably more what he deserved.

Will was still asleep. Nate didn't know what time his friend had come home; he'd slept soundly enough to miss it. After a shower, he started Will's coffee maker instead of reaching for a beer. A token effort to get his act together. If they wanted to see him, he didn't want to be drunk or hungover, though that probably wasn't too unusual in this line of work. Who interviewed for someone to break horses, anyway? The straight farm job he could understand, but usually exercise riders from the track picked up this kind of work because they could gallop in the mornings and do the babies in the afternoon; make a little extra cash. Maybe the place was suspect. There had to be a reason no one wanted to start their horses. Nothing ventured, though. If the place turned out to be a freak show, he could say no. Assuming they'd even want him.

When Will surfaced, looking the way Nate had felt too many mornings of late — rumpled and absolutely hungover — Nate was leaning back in a chair, quietly plucking the strings of one of Will's guitars. Will had a keyboard, but Nate hadn't touched it. He hadn't touched keys in any fashion since the new year had rolled in.

He stilled the strings and grinned at his friend. "Coffee's on."

Will raised an eyebrow, squinting with the effort of it, and frowned with suspicion, like he didn't quite recognize the guy with the guitar; a vague memory from his teenage years when it was a normal sight. He shuffled to the kitchen and poured himself a cup before shuffling to the couch.

"You're awfully chipper this morning," Will growled. "Sorry about last night. Not much of a friend, letting you leave your own birthday celebration while I partied."

Nate shrugged. "Don't worry about it. Glad one of us enjoyed it. What time do you have to work today?"

"Eleven. Which is soon enough. Guess I don't have to worry about you anymore?"

"Well... not sure about that, but don't worry about me, just the same."

Will's laugh was a half-grunt. "I'll leave you to that, then.

I'd better get ready."

After Will left, Nate kicked around the apartment. He should probably go out, take a walk, get some fresh air, if big-city smog even remotely resembled that, but this space was like a cocoon. So he stayed, picking at the guitar some more, then fingering through Will's books, finding something to read. How long had it been since he'd just sat and read a book?

Of course, he checked his email incessantly. The doubts grew. The track was where he was meant to be. He should accept that; pursue it with conviction. But he wasn't sure anymore that he wanted that dream without her.

It was late afternoon when he got the email through the job site.

Dear Mr Miller:

Thank you for your application. Are you free to come for an interview at 1pm tomorrow?

Sincerely,

Olivia

He almost laughed at the formality of it, but he didn't hesitate to respond immediately, doubts gone.

Dear Olivia: (might as well keep up the formality. There was no job title, or he would have gone with that).

Thanks for your response. I am.

Respectfully,

Nate Miller

Within minutes, he received the follow-up with the farm's address. Triple Stripe Stables. The name made his heart skip a beat. While not a huge outfit, you couldn't be a Canadian in the sport of horse racing and not know who they were. They had bred, campaigned, and now stood as a stallion Just Lucky, a horse who had won the Canadian Triple Crown three years ago, the first since early in the millennium. A horse the entire country had adored and cheered for. That didn't happen often with Canadian racing anymore. How great would it be to get in with such a place?

This interview was his shot to prove his worth, though he might have to do some play-acting to convince himself — let alone this Olivia — he could be any kind of asset.

There were no dreams of nightmare farms lingering when he woke the next morning. No dreams at all that he could recall. Maybe that was appropriate. He left Will's apartment before his friend was up, too fidgety to stay in one spot.

He was curious, and let the GPS direct him to Woodbine. The towering grandstand was visible from the 427 highway, on the opposite side from the Toronto airport, and he almost pulled over to take in the elevated view. The off-ramp fed directly into the turning lane that took him into acres of parking lot. There were still fields at the west end. That land had to be worth a chunk of change, but he'd read bits and pieces of the big plans they had for the property. Some kind of hotel/gaming/entertainment/residential complex.

Racing was surviving rather than thriving in Ontario. It had taken a hit when the lucrative Slots At Racetracks Program had ended. Still, it was doing better than Alberta, despite recent attempts to revive things. Which is why he was supposed to be here.

You'll outgrow this place, his boss, Al Wilson, had told him.

You owe it to yourself to go. I can't hold you back, his ex had insisted.

Apparently, they both believed in him more than he believed in himself. Being here seemed like it was under duress. In the end, he'd left Calgary because he felt he had no choice. His future there had been dead in the water. He had to create a new one here.

The cars presently in the parking lot weren't there to watch horse racing, because there wasn't any this afternoon. They were there for the casino. Did their presence help or hurt the sport of kings? He followed the signs for the stable area, catching only a peek of the actual racetrack surface.

He pulled onto the shoulder near the entrance, close enough to glimpse the security trailer and booth with a barrier that prevented anyone from driving straight into the stable area. No unauthorized access. He glanced at the crumpled scrap of paper Al had given him. A couple of names and numbers; people who might sign him in, sign his application, if not give him a job, as a favour to their old friend Al.

The prospect of being a freelance exercise rider in a place where no one knew him was intimidating. He wasn't the person Al and Cindy thought he was. But he needed to work, and that's what he was qualified to do. Not that he was any less qualified to be a hotwalker, cooling horses out after they trained. When it came down to it, a paycheque was a paycheque. Walking horses was just a much smaller one. It would let him keep a low profile, though. It might be just the thing if push came to shove. But how long would it last? How long before someone figured him out? Play-acting intentions aside, he wasn't sure he'd be convincing in the role of an inexperienced hack. With horses, true colours had a way of showing.

He watched for a while. Watched cars drive up to the security booth, cards scanned, barrier lifted to allow them through; watched a truck and trailer with stomping cargo roll to a stop, the driver showing credentials, speaking with the guard. Watched one get turned away and directed to the trailer. There was no sneaking into the Woodbine backstretch, though the guard didn't check the horse van for stowaways.

The long, two-story red brick building to the left of the road into the stable area was a dormitory. Maybe he could get a room there, though at the height of the racing season, it was probably full. Gone were the days of living in tack rooms on the backstretch, but he would have been up for that. He'd lived in the near equivalent of one on Al's farm from January until a few days ago. Popping the gearshift into first, he let the GPS lady lead him away. He'd put his aspirations on ice so long ago now, he was having trouble warming them up again. Too bad he'd failed to put his heart in the same place.

Minor roads took him north. Up Highway 27, which wasn't really a highway compared to the 400-system roads. East on King Sideroad. He pulled over when he made it to King City and went into a small coffee shop.

It was plain. There was nothing on the drab walls and only a few small tables with chairs that didn't exactly invite sit-down guests. Neither did the woman behind the counter. She was shorter than him, but terrifying, glowering under dark brows and matching tight-knit curls. Kind of an evil step-twin of his own blonde, sweet mother. He pressed his lips together so he didn't laugh out loud.

"Are you Lucy?" he ventured. The sign on the shop had said Lucy's Café.

"You must not be from around here," she snapped. "What can I get you?"

Order and move on, chump.

He came away with coffee and a butter tart and sat in his

car. One bite of the butter tart and he was in heaven. Under that gruff exterior, Lucy — if that frightful creature had been Lucy — was an angel. It would come in handy to have one in his court if he got the job. You could find them in the most unsuspecting places.

CHAPTER SIX

SHE WAS NERVOUS. Sweating. Her palms, her armpits. She needed to find something to do, so she appeared occupied when the prospect arrived, but it would just be busywork. She tried opening a textbook but was too distracted to focus.

Face it head on, then. She scanned his application, reading over the cover letter and resumé she'd printed out. There were questions, of course, that came to mind. Why come east? He'd worked for a trainer in Calgary. On the farm. Galloping. And he'd completed a year and a half at the University of Calgary. Did he flunk out? Why apply for a farm job instead of going to the track? He'd make better money there. His cover letter was vague, not naming the exact position he was applying for. She wasn't Human Resources for some corporation, but she liked it when people followed rules. He hadn't.

With any luck, she could at least fill the position for the yearlings. Then all she'd have to do would be to decide who she should interview for the general farm job. Most of the applicants were female, young women just out of high school who thought they wanted to make a living in the horse business.

Young women with dreams. Young women not unlike her and the staff currently employed on the farm. Ones who'd convinced their parents it was what they wanted to do, even though it meant a life living under the poverty line, or who defied the common sense doled out by their elders. At least she was trying to conform.

The sound of the barn door opening put her back on edge, and she straightened non-existent things on the desk, glanced over her shoulder at the big oil painting hanging behind her as if garnering moral support — Geai standing between her father's two best horses, Just Lucky and Sotisse — and wished she hadn't agreed to do this. It should be Geai sitting here.

It was Emilie's voice she heard, chattering away easily. Emilie would be good at this job. Emilie liked talking to people.

Her sister pushed the door open. She looked slightly flushed, her eyes a touch brighter than usual, a grin on her face as she met Liv's eyes, holding them for a second before speaking. "Hey Liv. Your guy's here."

Liv tried not to let her brows knot at her sister's expression. *Not my guy.* "Thanks, Em," she said, attempting to keep her voice light and professional, but it came out with a pointy bite.

"Nice to meet you," Emilie said as she motioned someone toward the door. "Good luck."

Good luck? Emilie's amused tone only heightened Liv's suspicion. She pasted on what she hoped was a pleasant smile, one that would convince a prospective employee luck would be unnecessary in the upcoming interview. When she raised her eyes, she was distracted a beat by Emilie, standing behind the man, giving a thumbs-up with one hand and pointing at his back with the other before she disappeared. *Damn it, Emilie.* As if she needed to be more flustered.

Then all that was left to look at was Nate Miller. Emilie

had disrupted her composure, and settling her eyes on him did nothing to restore it.

Guys didn't get to her. They didn't make her breath shorten or her heart race. Only a horse could do that. She left those things to other girls. She'd skipped that stage — the teenage crushes, celebrity idols — because she knew famous people were just as human as everyone else.

She blamed the way her nerve endings came to life on the fact that she spent so little time around men her age. Her class at school was predominantly female and the only male she might consider attractive was a jerk who was not difficult to disdain. But oh, the farm's all-female staff was going to go on and on about this guy in front of her. If she hired him, that was.

Blond. Even from across the room, she could tell his eyes were blue. Wary, though. Unsure. Probably because of the stupid look on her own face. She rubbed her damp palms on her jeans, tucked an imaginary strand of hair behind her ear, and forced herself to her feet.

"Come in." Her tongue tripped over the words.

He had to know he was attractive, but she tried to watch him as she would a yearling at the sales. He had a good walk. He was well put-together; a stayer, lithe and lean, not a bulky sprinter. She snapped her eyes back up from where they'd drifted.

You were checking him out, Liv. Admit it. Get over it. She reached across the desk, offering her hand; needing the boundary of the big old chunk of oak. His grip matched hers: firm, damp.

"Have a seat." She swept an arm toward the old overstuffed chair set in front of the expansive block of wood.

As she watched him sit, it struck her how ludicrous it was that she was in this position. She'd never even had a job interview herself. The only time she'd ever had to convince someone she was worthy of consideration was when she'd applied to vet school, an experience she didn't care to remember. Somehow her introvert self had muddled through the terrifying process, and she'd still been accepted, so she must not have messed up too much. Those connections some of her classmates goaded her about had probably helped.

Any of the "jobs" she'd had, she'd assumed. At her grandfather's farm, cleaning stalls and tacking up her own pony was expected. He didn't believe in babying. When her family had moved to this farm, she'd never expected special treatment for being the owner's daughter. She pitched in when she could, weekends and after school. She didn't identify her status; the help found out from someone else. As would Nate Miller, though, thanks to her sister, he might already know.

She was aware she'd been silent too long. He waited, a slight lift to one eyebrow, not smiling, but not looking unpleasant, either. It was her responsibility to lead this thing. She needed to step up. She lifted his resumé from the desk and ran her eyes over it, giving herself another moment to compose herself. Had she even introduced herself? Did she need to? Probably a good idea.

"Thanks for coming. I'm Liv." No need to volunteer more than that. She didn't have an official title, after all.

"Nice to meet you," he said. His hands rested on his thighs, though they weren't still. Maybe he was nervous too? "Thanks for seeing me."

His expression remained guarded. She kind of liked that, too. Too often guys could be smarmy, especially the good-looking ones. He wasn't looking at her like he thought she was too young, either. He seemed respectful. One point in the win column, then.

She was far too accustomed to others making assumptions about her age to do so with someone else, but she'd already made a good guess because of when he'd attended high school. Still, there was something careworn about his features that made him seem older than that number — which was close to her own.

"I'm assuming you want to ride races," she said, dropping her gaze to the paper again. She envied that he'd left university behind; envied his freedom to just not go back to school in September. His conviction to come east and pursue a dream — the same dream she had herself, but wasn't at liberty to follow.

He looked taken aback. *What, no small talk?*

No. Sorry.

"Uh — yeah, eventually. I've only been in Ontario for a few days. I figure I'll take some time to get to know some people first. It's not as if I was riding out west."

She almost laughed. Because a guy like that — that looked like that, was that good-looking, with eyes so blue even she couldn't ignore them — should not be stammering. If she used words like *adorable*, as if she were a girl in a teen movie, which she most definitely was not, she would do so right now. But she did not. She'd leave it to the farm staff to fawn over him — and fawn over him they would. If she hired him.

She recomposed herself. "So you only worked for the one trainer out there?"

"Not exactly. They only have so many days of Thorough-bred racing at Century Downs. They race everything there — Quarter Horses and Standardbreds too. Al — my employer — trained a few Quarter Horses as well. But he only had so many horses, so this past year I got on some for other trainers, too. Even helped out with the Standardbreds. I was just happy to be around the horses, regardless of breed."

"But you never rode. Races, I mean," she added, even though he'd already told her that. At Woodbine, a rider was a race-rider. When a trainer said they'd put a rider up to work a horse in the morning, it meant a jockey, instead of an exercise rider. Did the same lingo extend to Alberta? She'd never paid much attention to the track outside of Calgary — Century Downs. It seemed like a mish-mash, running all three breeds. How did trainers survive?

Nate shook his head. "No."

He didn't expand, and she didn't ask. He was taller than average for a jockey — and not riding weight at the moment — but with his light build, he could probably get there, so it likely wasn't his weight that was the issue. At his age, it wasn't as if he was going to grow or bulk up.

"Are you galloping for someone at the track in the morning?" She should clarify which position he was applying for, not just assume.

"Uh, no." That hesitation again. Insecurity? She read animals so much better than people. "I'm not afraid of turning out and doing stalls too, if that's what's required."

His words were earnest. *Cute.* Again, she pushed aside the thought. She didn't concern herself with cute.

"So you're interested in the farm job? Not just the yearlings? I hope it doesn't offend you to point out you're probably grossly over-qualified."

"Is anyone actually ever over-qualified to muck stalls?"

It was only the quickest of glimpses, but he flashed her a dazzling grin that almost made her duck, the way it sucked the breath from her lungs and made her skin warm. Dangerous. Just as briefly, she let herself imagine a simpler version of herself, like one of her younger sister's romance novels, where the owner's daughter fell for the new farm hand. Then she had to stop herself from snorting with laughter. She needed to maintain professionalism here.

"You don't want to start yearlings?" she asked, still trying to clarify.

"I could do both. If you'd consider that. I don't mind if it means working with the babies after the rest of the work is done."

She suppressed a smile at the thought of no more interviews. No more reviewing the pile of applications. She'd have to run it past Geai, of course...

"Truth is," he said before she had a chance to respond, "I'm looking for a place to live. The job posting said accommodations are available."

"There are," she said. "The apartment's just upstairs. I'll show you."

It was a relief to move, until she started up the stairs, aware of him following — more than just because of the sound of his shoes on the steps. She glanced over her shoulder — he was a respectable distance behind her. It was almost too generous a space, following with his head down, though he wasn't grasping the railing, so she didn't think it was because he was watching his step, literally or figuratively. He was just stuck in his own head. Which was interesting. Or would be interesting, if she were interested.

She opened the door — it wasn't locked — and stood aside. He passed her with a quick glance before he started scanning the walls. They were bare, the same warm museum white as the living room at the house because there'd been leftover paint. The floor was engineered hardwood, a medium-brown she couldn't identify because she never paid attention to those things. If it had been a horse, she'd call it dun. She didn't know what kind of wood it was supposed to be. Decorating was her mother's department. It looked nice, though. At least she thought it did.

It was sparsely furnished — a couch, an armchair, a TV stand. The kitchen had a microwave. The bedroom had a bed. But his gaze went to the picture window — which dominated the room — and when he wandered over to it, his eyes dropped to the old upright piano beneath it. He hesitated as he stared at it with what almost looked like longing, or regret. She looked away as he caressed it.

"Is it in tune?" he asked. Like when he'd made the quip about being over-qualified, she saw a tiny view of his character. He lost some of his mask.

"I have no idea, but I seriously doubt it." She almost thought he was going to hit a few keys to find out, but he didn't.

"It's a great space."

He opened the door to the bedroom and peeked in, then did the same for the bathroom. The whole time, she remained by the door. It wasn't a lengthy inspection, but it still seemed to her to take forever. He stopped a good six feet from her and jammed his hands in his pockets, so she stepped away from the door again, letting him pass through. And this time, she followed him down the stairs. There was nothing to do but look at his descending figure — lean, fit. Nice shoulders and arms. An easy way of going complicated by an underlying disquiet.

At the bottom of the stairs, he stood aside. She hesitated, then returned to the office, assuming her place behind the desk and waiting while he went to the chair.

Were there other things she should ask? She'd googled "interview questions" but the results seemed appropriate for a corporate environment, not a horse farm. Horse farms usually just handed you a lead or a pitchfork, and how you handled either quickly revealed what may or may not have been with-held. The apartment, though, added a layer. It wouldn't be good to promise it and have the person bolt a few days later or have to both fire and evict them. If she could devise a question that would determine the likelihood of him sticking around, she'd have something worthwhile. Asked straight out, of course he'd say that was his plan. Anyone would.

She glanced over the resumé again, just to look thoughtful. "You're comfortable with basic first aid? For the horses, I mean. Though if you can do the same for people, I guess that would be a bonus."

He seemed to smother a laugh. "Horses, yes."

"Injections?"

"I'm fine with IM." Intramuscular. "I've never done IV."

"It's easy. I'm sure you'd learn quickly." If he'd watched it as many times as she had, all it took was the decision to just do it. Plump the jugular vein, set the needle at the appropriate angle, slip it in. The racehorses were good first-time subjects. They were so used to it, they stood like champs.

"So — if that happened, if you did both, you wouldn't get special treatment because you're an exercise rider. You and Geai — he's the farm manager — would have to figure out when you did the yearlings, because the barn work comes first. And if you're living here, Geai might ask you to feed or water off sometimes, like on his day off. He does most of it the other days, but having someone else around would give him a break."

"Not a problem," he said. "I'm happy to help in any way I can."

"Most of the hay is off now, but there's a bit of second cut left to do. Everyone helps with hay. And sometimes you might have to cut grass." He just nodded as she babbled on. "Sometimes we have post-op horses and a bit of rehab to do. Can you put on a bandage?"

"Yes."

Can you do it well? She wanted to ask. But this was a farm hand job he thought he wanted. He wasn't taking his trainer's test. It wasn't a requirement of the job; it would just be handy.

"With the yearlings, we're not in a big hurry to get them going. It's more important they get a good foundation. You know — actually learn how to steer. And be confident. Geai will be the one on the ground. He's great. All the yearlings raised here are pretty well-handled, but sometimes we get a couple sent to us that aren't so much."

"How many homebreds?" he asked.

"Three. Two colts, one filly. There are two others for sure, and could be more after the sale next week." Another nod. "I'll have to talk to Geai about the wage, because you'd be paid more than just what you'd get for the straight farm position. Also, the farm job actually includes benefits and you get statutory holidays. You might not actually get them off, but you'll be compensated for them."

One of his eyebrows crept up. "You're kidding, right?"

"No. My father is a businessman, and he's very fair." Well — she'd let that slip out.

"That's great."

Another awkward silence fell between them as she figured out what was next. She hated feeling this ill-prepared. This was just one of those things you had to learn by doing, she supposed.

A tour of the farm was a logical next-step. Did it have to be her? Emilie was probably lurking, waiting to hear how it went, to catch another glimpse of the potential new guy. Liv keyed in a text, feeling Nate's eyes on her, waiting. She was aware of being rude, but finished the message to her sister, anyway. *Can I impose upon you to give our prospect a tour?*

Emilie's response came immediately. *At your service!* With a string of laughing emojis.

Yeah. Thought so.

"Sorry about that," she said, controlling her features as she lifted her eyes from the phone. "I've got a few things to catch up on here, so I hope you don't mind that my sister's going to take you around to see the farm. She'll introduce you to the manager. She should be here in a moment." Would that offend

him? Did she care? Geat would catch anything she'd missed. "Do you have any questions for me?"

There was only a slight hesitation before he responded. "Just one. Why don't you already have someone? Kinda late in the game, isn't it?"

She paused, deciding how to answer, and went with honesty. "It's taken me this long to accept I can't do it myself."

He didn't ask what she meant by that, and she didn't explain. There was maybe even a trace of a smile on his lips. Score another point for this guy.

Emilie appeared in the doorway, and Nate followed Liv's gaze as she met her sister's eyes. Again, she had to control her expression, Emilie's all bright and mischievous.

"Come with me," Emilie said with her welcoming smile. She'd balance out Liv's stiffness.

Nate stood, but paused. "Nice to meet you."

Liv scrambled to her feet when he offered his hand, her nerves tripping her up. "Likewise," she responded, pressing her lips together and deciding she didn't enjoy being an interviewer any more than being an interviewee.

She liked him all right, though. Not because of his looks — his looks were a liability — but he seemed good at minding his own business. All offerings were on a need to know basis. It set the stage nicely for their relationship.

She wouldn't be around much.

They wouldn't become friends.

It was perfect.

CHAPTER SEVEN

HAD HE JUST BEEN DISMISSED? Passed off like an inconvenient child? No matter. The sister seemed like more fun, anyway. Not that he was here to have fun, but no one liked a tense work environment. You know, if he was even up for consideration. He couldn't tell.

Up in the apartment — which was great — she'd stayed by the door like she thought he was going to jump her. He'd almost told her he was the last guy on earth she had to worry about. Not that she wasn't attractive. He'd give her that much, even if she had a bug permanently up her cute butt.

The sister was, from his brief assessment, completely the opposite of Liv. Not in appearances, because while he guessed there was a difference in their ages, just because of their mannerisms and the way they talked, the resemblance between them was strong. Both of them were striking, with long dark hair and blue eyes, though Liv's were closer to grey — or maybe that's just how he'd pegged them because of her standoffish personality. But where Liv was serious, closed off in a way that was unsettling, almost, this sister was, in comparison, carefree.

"What was your name again?" It embarrassed him to have to ask, but might as well be forthright.

"Emilie. And don't worry, I doubt Liv even told you. She's bad that way."

"I'm Nate," he said, not wanting to assume she knew.

"You're from Calgary?" she asked.

"Yeah. First time in Ontario."

"You drove? How long did that take? I'd love to go cross-country sometime. What do you think of Ontario so far?"

He almost laughed at her stream of questions. So far? So far Ontario was highway and a big city on a big lake. And humid. Out here impressed him more. Lots of green, gently rolling hills, though not a mountain in sight. Pretty farm, pretty horses, pretty girls.

"That coffee shop in town is a gem," he said.

"Lucy's? Oh my gosh," Emilie gushed. "Best butter tarts in the province. Did you have one? So worth actually dealing with Lucy."

He'd guessed right, then. He grinned. "So it wasn't just me? Good to know."

They strode along a wide stone dust lane that was in better condition than the dirt sideroad he'd driven on to get here, a freshly painted white fence line on the left and pale grey outbuildings with blue trim on the right. A couple of tractors were parked inside one, the other stuffed with hay, still fresh enough for him to catch the sweet scent of timothy and alfalfa. Just ahead, tall evergreens clustered on both sides of the lane, their verdant boughs overlapping, and beyond, on the left, was a long, low barn — matching the others, of course — its dutch doors open.

"I'll show you around," she said, "then take you to Geai. You'll love him. Everyone does. I'm sure Liv told you that you'd be working with him for starting yearlings. You couldn't have a better person on the ground." She barely took a breath as she continued. "There are three regular farm staff. One is going back to school, which is why we're hiring someone new. She'll probably still come on weekends to help on days off and such."

They walked up to the barn, and she paused outside the doors.

"This is where the yearlings will be. There's a sand ring right there." She pointed to the obvious outdoor riding area. "Indoor arena attached to the barn, so you can keep them going if the weather's bad."

He followed her into the dark aisle. The stalls were all empty, neatly mucked and bedded.

"Tack room — which is also the break room," she motioned to a door on the left. "Feed room at the end. When we have layups or post-ops, they're in here, but no one is on stall rest right now. It's just a matter of learning the routine, right? From what I understand, you have more experience than a lot of people who have worked here did when they started. I'm sure you can handle it."

She swept out of the training barn and he walked a half-pace behind her, not quite royal consort distance.

"Weanlings are over here — boys in one pasture, girls in another. They live outside right now. We banished their mommas to the other side of the farm. We're past the pitiful whinnies stage, thank goodness. I hate that so much. It breaks my heart every time!"

Tour guide, Welcome Wagon, ambassador... and softie. It was hard not to like this kid. While he still kept the same distance between himself and her that he had with Liv, carrying himself with a similar caution, it gradually wore off as Emilie performed her duty — which didn't come off as duty at all.

"There's an Instagram page. I guess I could have just given you that and saved you the time." She grinned.

Of course there was an Instagram page. And he was sure it was Emilie's project.

"Naw. This is better." He smiled, but kept it restrained. He could too easily get sucked into flirting with this one. "But I'm surprised your sister didn't do that," he added dryly. It slipped. He slid her a glance.

She laughed. "So am I."

Emilie didn't expand on her amusement, though. He could tell she was dying to. Give it time. He knew who to butter up if he needed information. The other one? The same tactic would be totally ineffective. Offensive, even.

The farm was gorgeous. From the maple-lined lane that had welcomed him, the flower beds he'd passed near what he assumed was the family home, to the neat white rail fencing everywhere, cut lawns and well-maintained barns. All of it was too good to be true. This farm, the apartment, the statutory holidays and benefits. He didn't dare imagine himself here... but he was doing just that.

"We can take a shortcut through the woods, if that's okay with you. There's a trail." Emilie glanced at his shoes. "It's dry. You'll be okay."

There was energy and abandon in her stride, her pace fast enough to make him work — he was sweating from the effort, having to think about his breathing. It was ridiculous how easily he'd lost fitness in his last month of languishing. Pathetic.

He was glad he hadn't worn boots, with all this walking. It wasn't as if he'd expected to get on a horse, at least not on the first visit. And Emilie clearly didn't have the same trust issues Liv did. She wasn't afraid of him following her into the thick grove of trees.

"This would be a great place to run." If he got the job and

moved out here, he'd get back into shape. He liked this farm better and better with every step.

"Liv runs through here all the time. We hack the horses here too, so just be aware there are sometimes, ah, obstacles."

The silence that fell between them lacked the awkwardness it had with Liv. It was peaceful in here. Soothing. Rejuvenating, like the trees performed their photosynthesis with mindfulness, infusing new life. A fresh start. Why ever would he want to work at Woodbine, breathing Toronto smog, when he could live here? Forever, maybe. He wanted forever, somewhere.

The wooded area gave way to a clearing, with a cottage on the left, another grey and blue barn beyond it, and in front of them, high-fenced paddocks. A driveway went right around the barn in a big loop.

"That's Geai's house, then the stallion barn and breeding shed." Emilie fell back into tour guide mode. She led the way to a paddock. There were four, two of them occupied.

A compact dark bay horse lifted his head from where he'd been grazing and charged over, his white legs flashing as they reached and bunched, closing the space rapidly. Emilie didn't flinch, but Nate was ready to grab her and get her out of the way, envisioning the horse crashing into the fence, sending rails flying everywhere. The stallion had good brakes, though, screeching to a halt just shy of the barrier. Then he tilted his head and pressed his whiskery pink muzzle to the space between the rails, which was barely wide enough for his nose. He huffed with noisy breaths — scenting, searching, expectant.

"You're such a dork," Emilie said, touching his nose briefly before withdrawing her hand with what appeared to be a healthy respect for the possibility of losing a finger. "This is Just Lucky. He's —"

"I know who he is," Nate interrupted, smiling. He resisted

the temptation to push his own palm to the stallion's nose. "Canadian Triple Crown winner. Expecting his first crop next year, right?"

"Right," Emilie said. She didn't look impressed that he knew. It likely would have been a ding against him if he hadn't.

"My father's pride and joy. And his favourite mare, Sotisse —"

"Canadian Oaks winner, second by a hair to Just Lucky in the Plate, second to Chibop in the EP Taylor."

"Yup. She's in foal to him. Due late January. We're kind of excited about that one."

"I guess." Who wouldn't be?

The stallion switched up his tactics, craning his head over the top rail. He wasn't very big, so there was no hope of him reaching either of them. He looked like he'd take a chomp given the opportunity, a cheeky glint in the eyes on either side of the crooked stripe that trailed down his face and widened into a large snip.

"He's a brat," Emilie said, with clear affection, then started walking again. "That one is Starway."

The other stallion, also dark bay but with no obvious white, didn't bother to lift his head from his mowing.

"First crop hit the races this year. A handful of winners so far," Nate recited. Starway was larger than Just Lucky, with more of a classic stayer look to him. Not that Just Lucky's bulky frame had kept him from winning at a mile and a half.

"You've done your homework." Emilie's grin was almost as cheeky as Just Lucky's expression had been.

So maybe he'd checked out the farm's website once he'd known that was where he was going.

"Come on," she said. "There's Geai."

The figure waiting outside the stallion barn, arms crossed, was a human version of Just Lucky. Not a tall man. Compact.

47

Stocky. Next to him waddled an old black Labrador with a greying muzzle. It was a definite case of dog and owner looking alike, except at the moment, the dog looked a lot friendlier. *Everybody loves Geai?* The Lab lumbered over, breaking into a trot that looked like a lot of work. The manager remained where he was.

"Napoleon!" Emilie cried, her intonation of the name French — the only indication she'd given of her heritage. She leaned over to thump the Lab's well-padded ribcage. "This is Napoleon."

Nate crouched to greet the black dog, burying his hands in the thick black neck rolls as Napoleon slathered him with his pink tongue. He laughed, grateful for a reason to put off a formal introduction to the man with the gruff stance. But when he looked up, Geai was right there, close enough for Nate to notice the lines on the manager's tanned face, the silvery scruff and sideburns, the crinkle in the corners of his eyes — and the subtle wry curve of his lips. Not that Nate felt he wasn't being completely scrutinized; it was just in a less intense way than he'd been by Liv.

He straightened his legs, glad when he didn't fall over, and offered his hand. "Nate Miller."

The man reciprocated. "Geai Doucet."

"Good luck," Emilie said again and touched his arm lightly as she left.

Did he need luck here, too? He felt like a baton being passed from one runner to the next.

"I won't keep you long," the old man started. Unlike the two young women, his accent was pronounced. "I'm sure Livvy has been thorough."

Yes, and no. She'd gone on about the riding thing a bit too much. He'd felt like saying *enough, already.* Though in hindsight, it hadn't seemed to be about him at all.

And, *Livvy?* That was cute. He couldn't imagine anyone getting away with calling her that. This Geai must get special consideration.

"You have plans to become a jockey?" Geai began.

Did they have to do this? Had she texted Geai a novel while Nate and Emilie were doing the tour? He needed to get them to let that go.

"Well — no immediate plans."

"And you really want to work on the farm too?"

"I'm not afraid of farm work." *I need to get off Will's couch.*

"What kind of assurance can you give us you won't pack your things and leave once the yearlings have finished their sixty days?"

How to answer that? How honest to be? How heart-felt? *Because I need a place to belong. A place to rewrite myself.*

"Well... giving me that apartment would be a considerable vote of confidence on your part. I understand that. It seems only fair that I honour that with a commitment beyond sixty days." Was that enough? Could he be that guy again? The one who craved that kind of relationship, even if it was just with a... farm?

Geai crossed his arms again, his eyes steady under brows more grey than black. Nate couldn't tell if he was passing the preliminary tests or not. He missed Emilie with her freely shared emotions.

"Why Triple Stripe?" Geai asked, then.

Not "why not Woodbine." The question presented was easier than that one.

"Because it would be an honour to work for an outfit like this. This horse over here, for one. That mare carrying his foal. That foal. A small outfit that produces quality. Who wouldn't want to work with horses like that?"

Geai looked satisfied, pausing a beat before continuing.

"The yearlings won't start until after Labour Day, but when would you be prepared to begin, if we decide to hire you for the farm position as well?"

Yesterday, he almost said. "Any time."

Geai nodded. "I'll leave you to find your way back to your car. Feel free to walk around. If you go down the lane," he motioned to his left, "it will lead you past the training track. Turn right when you see the house and that will take you back to the office."

He felt conspicuous as he returned to the Mustang, especially as he passed the main residence. It was hard to see much of it; the backyard enclosed by a privacy fence, the house surrounded by a variety of trees and colourful gardens. But no one came out to accost him. Everyone seemed to have gone back into hiding. It might just be that time of day. Were they watching him from somewhere? Did a place like this have cameras everywhere?

He wondered if Liv or Emilie would appear from the barn, but there was no sign of anyone. He paused a moment once he was inside the Mustang, grasping the wheel. Liv was a bit weird, but otherwise, he liked the feel of this place. Of course, his instincts could be all off. They'd let him down recently.

He couldn't help going back to the café in town, those butter tarts calling his name. He'd take some back to Will. Lucy didn't make any comment about his reappearance; she just served up the half-dozen he ordered with the same gruff efficiency.

"Thanks," he said, then added with a note of hope, "See you around."

CHAPTER EIGHT

"You're going to hire that one, right?" Emilie plunked herself down on the chair in front of the desk.

Liv laughed, her sister's reaction no surprise. "I'm going to check his references and talk to Geai." Should they do a background check, too? Maybe he'd done something in Calgary that had made him leave. Maybe he was running from something. "Do you think we should see him on a horse?" Not everyone who galloped horses was good at it.

"Who cares if he can ride when he looks like that? We need some eye candy around here."

"Not sure you get a vote, Em. Besides, school starts soon. When will you have the pleasure of taking advantage of that?"

"I'll live for weekends." Emilie grinned.

As will I, for entirely different reasons, she thought. Galloping in the mornings, afternoons with Claire.

"Seriously, though," her sister continued. "He's very nice, right? Polite. Didn't put a foot wrong."

"Maybe it's an act. A bit too good to be true."

"You would think that, Miss Glass Half-Empty. Besides, if

he was going to put on an act, don't you think he'd be a little, you know, cheerier?"

"You noticed that too? I thought it was just me."

"No, he was definitely, I don't know... broody, almost. Which just made him more delicious."

Liv rolled her eyes. "He might be too much of a distraction around here, if your reaction is any indication. Our great crew might not get any work done."

"Sure they will. They'll be trying to out-do each other to either impress him or finish faster so they can have longer coffee breaks."

"I've only scratched the surface of the applicants."

"Let's see the others. I could use a laugh."

Emilie peered over Liv's shoulder at the computer screen as Liv went through them. There were more than a couple that made her wonder. Some Emilie was sure she knew and gave a yea or nay. A few Liv made a note of to look at again.

Emilie pushed up from her bent stance and stretched. "Gotta go. Tell him if he needs any help to move in, I'm available."

"Sure, Em. See you later."

She watched her sister leave, then drew in a deep breath, psyching herself up to call the reference she figured carried the most weight — Al Wilson, the trainer Nate Miller had worked for out west. Best to get it done and see which way it swayed her thinking.

They still had a landline in each barn. It would look best if the caller ID came through with the farm name instead of her own. The guy would probably know the farm; her, not so much. He picked up after a couple of rings and she made her inquiry quickly.

"Nate's a good kid," Wilson told her. "He can sure as hell ride. He would have outgrown Century Downs in short order, though I could never talk him into getting his license here. And he's great with the babies. Give him a shot and you won't regret it. He needs a break. He needs something good to happen."

It was hard to stop herself from asking what that meant — and usually she had absolutely no problem keeping her mouth shut. If he was as experienced and talented as Al Wilson was suggesting, why wasn't he looking to get his apprentice license in short order? The excuse he'd offered was a little thin. What was holding him back? But he seemed all right, and Wilson seemed genuine in his praise. Really, what did it matter if he was overqualified? All she should be thinking was that she had lucked out in finding someone decent to help with the yearlings. All the better if he wanted a permanent position on the farm. The women would have their eye candy, and Geai would have some extra muscle.

It pushed her thoughts back to her own future. She'd latched onto the inevitability of pursuing a veterinary degree before she'd even hit high school. When the yearlings were starting their training, she'd be returning to her own education. It didn't matter that she wasn't sure it's what she really wanted, wasn't sure it was her true calling. Did everyone have one of those? Did everyone get to follow it?

Becoming a veterinarian was a practical career, combining her love of horses with her love of science. It grounded her, kept her brain stable. Gave her a schedule, consistency, routine. Too much time left to herself and she'd overthink everything, though she managed to do that anyway.

It niggled at her, though, with this new guy. She hated him a little — which might not be fair because he seemed decent enough. But he had the freedom to do what she really wanted to do. Ride races. And smart horse girls went to vet school, they didn't become jockeys.

Geai caught her looking reflectively at the wall next to the desk. The cabinet there wasn't packed like some trophy case in a movie. The items in it weren't props for a film set. They were real, live mementos of a dream executed. Her father's dream; the one she'd inherited. The thing that would always tie her to him, when in other ways they could be so awkward together, neither of them good at affection.

Not like Geai, who was the grandfather figure her blood relative had never been. It was Geai she associated with her earliest memories of horses at her grandfather's hunter/jumper farm. Geai had always been there. He'd taught her horsemanship. Her grandfather had merely given her riding lessons.

And Daniel Lachance had been the most demanding of instructors, but Liv had craved the perfection he insisted on — not because she cared about shows and ribbons, but because the more adept she became as a rider, the better partner she'd be. He'd recognized her drive, if not her motivation. Thankfully, Geai had recognized her love, and fostered it.

She owed him everything.

He dropped into the chair in front of the desk — the one Nate had sat in with the same unease she'd felt in her own chair. All of that slipped away with Geai.

"So?" He molded into the backrest, elbows draped over the arms. "What do you think?"

"He wants the apartment," she answered, like it was a problem.

"It makes sense if he's just moved here."

"Who just moves here without already having a place to live, though? It seems like such a gamble." Even if horse people did it all the time. That was the problem with horses. Following your heart had the potential to lead you astray.

"Says Miss Risk Averse. He could live in a hotel temporarily. Maybe he has a friend in the area. It's not unreasonable. Why are you trying to find reasons not to like him?"

"You do, then?"

"He seems like a good kid."

"I called the trainer he gave as a reference."

"And?"

"Nothing but good things." Could it be that simple? "The final decision isn't mine, anyway."

"Your input carries weight, though. If you have reason to think he's not a good fit, say so. You have other candidates to consider."

None of them like this one, though. He had the experience and the manner. His looks weren't a good reason to dismiss him. She sighed. "Is it wrong he seems too good a fit? Too good to be true?"

"Sometimes you have to take a chance on someone. Give someone a chance. Maybe that's what he needs."

"So you're saying Miss Risk Averse should give this guy a shot?" She eyed him with a wry twist of her lips.

She could be done with the interviews. Have the position settled so she could enjoy what time she had left of her summer break before plunging back into academics. Give Claire her full attention.

She'd wait until tomorrow morning to call him, though. Doing it right now felt too desperate, like they'd had so few possibilities for the position they had to jump on the first one they got. But could there be someone out there more perfect for the job?

Perfect. Was that even possible?

Short of actually getting a police check — which admittedly seemed obsessive — she'd done her due diligence, even if it hadn't given her any more clues. A Google search on Nate Miller had come up with nothing. No alarm bells, no red flags. The first few hits were definitely not him. Some fictional character on a show she hadn't been able to figure out the title of, and a lawyer in the States somewhere. All she'd found was his Facebook profile, and it was sparse. Some old photos others had tagged him in, which she kept herself from looking at for long because it made her feel like a stalker. There was nothing recent. Either he kept his privacy settings locked down, or didn't indulge in social media. His cover photo was of the mountains; his profile image a shot of him galloping a horse. She let herself study that. His position was great, balanced perfectly over the horse's centre of gravity, his eyes forward.

There it was again. Perfect.

Well, Mr Miller. Let's give this a shot.

CHAPTER NINE

HE MADE himself promise not to eat all the butter tarts, so there were some left for Will, who was at work by the time he got back. *You want to be a rider someday...* he pulled a flap of skin from his abdomen and wondered what his body fat percentage was now. Butter tarts would have to go if and when that day came, so might as well make the most of it now.

The groceries he'd picked up on his way back into the city had gone on his credit card because he was woefully low on cash. Something about the promise of income gave him hope he'd be able to pay off that bill when it came, even if the job wasn't his yet. He kicked off his shoes and carried the bags to the kitchen, made himself a salad from ingredients he'd bought — to balance the rich pastry — and sat at the circular table instead of the couch for a change.

While he ate, he did an Instagram search for the Triple Stripe account and scrolled through the snaps. It was well done. The kid had a good eye, and she'd taken the time to curate it with a warm palette and all those other things you were supposed to do. A far cry from his own account, which was one of those really sad ones: a grand total of three attempted artsy shots — his guitar, the Rockies and the family Golden Retrievers. He pushed away from the table and cleaned his dishes, then composed a shot of a butter tart on a plate to let cyberspace know he was still alive.

Next, he checked his email, in case there was something from the farm, even though that was probably ridiculous. It was far too soon. But maybe she'd send a "thanks for coming, we'll be in touch" message. She hadn't. Should he send something to reaffirm his interest? It couldn't hurt. He dashed it off quickly, proof-reading it three times to be sure it was okay before hitting send because Olivia Lachance was probably the type to take typos or grammatical errors personally. He'd hate to lose the job for something like that.

With Will gone, he didn't know what to do with himself, too distracted to get back into the book he'd started. He kept his phone charging to be sure the battery was topped up, staying within reach and obsessively checking the screen in case he missed a call or email.

Picking chords on one of Will's guitars, he thought about the piano in that apartment above the barn. It was a sign, wasn't it? That old piece of furniture was calling him. Taunting him, even. He hadn't played since he left home. And by home, he meant the house he'd grown up in; the one from which his father had evicted him long before he'd left Alberta.

What business had he had, really, asking anyone to marry him when he'd still been living under his parents' roof, eating their food? If he thought he'd been supporting himself working weekends for Al while he went to school full time, he'd been delusional. And he had been, completely and totally, about so much. *Idiot.* He'd never really lived on his own, just occupied a glorified tack room for almost eight months. That hardly counted.

He was afraid if he hoped too much, he'd scare this job away, but he longed for what it offered. Not the wage. Not the benefits or the statutory holidays. But the space — physical and emotional — to become whoever he was supposed to be.

———

He was sure Will didn't mean to wake him up, but he'd been sleeping so restlessly, he popped up from where he'd fallen asleep on the couch as soon as he heard the click of the door.

"Sorry," Will whispered.

"That's okay. What time is it?" He stretched, the words coming out in a yawn.

"I don't know. Two? How'd the interview go?" Will asked.

"Good. Gorgeous farm, gorgeous horses." He left out Liv and Emilie, though they certainly deserved the same adjective. "Even the possibility of a really nice apartment with the job."

"Did you get it? Hire you on the spot? Tell them to call me. I'll give you a glowing reference." Will grinned.

"Tired of me already?" Nate laughed, waking up. He didn't have to be up early so he could help Will decompress. "They'll let me know. I really hope I get it, though. I really like the place, and the people. The farm manager seems like a good guy. The owner has two daughters who seem to be involved in the place."

"There you go. That'll get Cindy out of your head. Think there's a job for me too? I can muck a stall."

"The one sister's too young and while the older one is definitely easy on the eyes, there's a whole 'look and don't touch' thing going on with her." He grinned, thinking even looking needed to be a covert thing with Liv Lachance. "But that's okay. Looking is enough. Touching just gets you burned."

"Only if you hold on." Will smacked him on the shoulder before wandering to the kitchen.

"Good point." Nate set the throw aside and followed him.

"Want a beer?" Will asked, opening the fridge.

"Does beer go with butter tarts?" He lifted the styrofoam tray he'd left next to the sink.

"Don't see why not. A maple-flavoured craft brew would be just the thing."

"You have that?"

Will laughed, handing him one of the same old red, white and blue-labeled brown bottles. "I do not."

"Canadian it is, then." Nate twisted off the cap and touched the neck of his bottle to Will's. "Are we celebrating again?"

Will shrugged. "Sure. Your job to be. Positive thinking and all that."

"Can't hurt," Nate decided.

The ringing of his phone jarred him out of the more settled sleep his late-night beer with Will had allowed him — keeping him under till eleven AM, apparently. He grappled for the device and saw the number. There it was. The farm. This could only mean good things, right? *Wake up, Miller.* But that would take longer than he had. He wasn't letting this call go to voicemail. When he answered, his voice was tentative, his throat rough.

"Hello?" he croaked. Great. He wasn't hungover, but he probably sounded like a deadbeat.

"Is this Nate?"

He thought he recognized the female voice, the slightest of

hesitations between *this* and *Nate* making him think she'd considered calling him Mr Miller again.

"It is." It came more like his own voice, and he tried to inject the right combination of confidence and friendliness into his tone.

"It's Liv Lachance from Triple Stripe. Would you be able to come one day for a working interview? If all goes well, the job is yours, if you want it. The apartment too."

Yes, yes, yes, yes, yes. Had she been standing in front of him, he'd have been tempted to kiss her, all that aloofness be damned. "Absolutely. Thank you."

"Seven AM Friday? Just go to the training barn. That's where everyone meets to start turning out."

"Thank you." He didn't care that he'd said it already. Thank you was one of those things it never hurt to repeat.

Working interview? He'd ace that. The job was as good as his.

CHAPTER TEN

IT WASN'T A LEISURE POOL, but that didn't stop Faye Taylor from stretching out on one of the nearby lounge chairs. "The summer is never long enough," she sighed.

"I'm ready to go back," Liv said, removing the elastic from her hair and toweling it dry before parking herself next to Faye to let the sun properly dry her off. It wasn't a lie, but she could see the curve of Faye's raised — and perfectly maintained — eyebrows above the rims of her sunglasses.

"Really?"

"Yes. Don't you just want to be done with school? The only way to make that happen is to get on with it."

"I suppose that's true, though I'd have more incentive if I had any clue what I was going to do after I graduate."

Faye didn't rehash the fact that Liv's future, on the other hand, was mapped out. All summer after galloping for her father's private trainer, Roger Cloutier, she'd helped Roger's track vet, Jake Monaghan. She didn't get to do much — she drew up syringes and held twitches and scrubbed up joints before they were injected — but she learned so much, both from Jake's generous sharing and from constant observation. That was what separated an exceptional vet from the average, wasn't it? Seeing the nuances, the subtle deviations from robust health. When she graduated, though it was unspoken, it was assumed she'd have a place in Jake's practice.

"You'll figure it out," Liv said.

"Or maybe I'll marry rich."

Unlike Liv, Faye could swing that, with her outgoing personality and easy fashion sense. She knew how to put on makeup — Liv had missed or avoided that mother-daughter lesson, never felt the need to teach herself, and Faye had long since declared her a lost cause. She always looked good in the flowy, feminine things Liv felt would be ridiculous on herself. And, most importantly, Faye could talk to anyone. Though Faye, best friend that she was, would never point out that Liv didn't need to marry rich. Of course, Liv didn't believe she needed to marry at all.

Her mother slipped through the sliding doors from the living room with a tray, not walking so much as gliding over to place a glass of something fizzy in Faye's hand and a plate of home-baked cookies on the small table between them. Because, of course. Liv pressed her lips together in a tight smile before raising her water bottle to her lips. She tried to take hospitality notes from her mother. Left to her, there would have been no refreshments for her guest. She hadn't inherited that particular gene from Anne Lachance. In fact, she was convinced all she'd inherited were physical ones: the dark hair, the bone structure, the slim build. Her grey eyes were her father's.

"Thanks, Anne," Faye said with a warm smile and slight lift of the glass before sipping. Anne nodded with a similar expression and disappeared back into the cool house. "Speaking of men..."

"Were we, actually?" Liv retorted. But it was a topic never

far from her best friend's mind. Liv reached for a cookie, which seemed like a good antidote to the subject.

"Emilie tells me..."

Here we go. Liv's eyes were rolling before the sentence was out of Faye's mouth.

"... you have a new employee. And, that he's rather attractive."

"She put it that way, did she?"

Faye snorted. "No. I think her exact words were, 'omygosh Faye, you have to see him, he is smoking hot.'"

Liv had to laugh at Faye's impersonation despite herself. "That sounds more like my sister. He's not on the payroll yet. He's doing a working interview today, just to be sure he knows which end of a pitchfork is which."

"Perhaps we should go see how he's doing?" Faye tilted her head slightly.

"I'm sure the current staff have that under control," Liv replied wryly.

"You're so boring. I already know he'd be perfect for you."

Liv choked on her water, and sputtered, "This guy you've never met and none of us really knows? How so?"

"He's good-looking and likes horses. I can't imagine you need any other boxes to check."

"Don't give up your career aspirations for matchmaking."

"Didn't we just agree I had no career aspirations? Clearly, he's not rich enough for me, so it's up to you."

"When would I have time for a relationship?"

"You make time for the important things, sweetie."

That one was way down the list. Like at the bottom, if it was even there.

"Besides," Faye continued, "who said I was talking about a relationship? A late-summer fling is exactly what you need."

Flings were Faye's bailiwick, and usually involved more

than willing young jockeys at the track who were resilient enough not to be wounded by her disdain for attachment of any sort.

"Right," Liv said. "Let's scare away the new guy right off."

"You're not that scary ."

She gave Faye a quick glance — that brief acknowledgement that her friend understood she was not whole.

To an outsider, their friendship would appear unlikely; the ultimate odd couple. She and Faye had met on Liv's first day of high school in Ontario — on the bus. Liv had refused her mother's offer to drive her, four months shy of being old enough to drive herself.

Faye, she learned, lived just down the road from the Lachance's new farm on her own family's farm, Northwest. Faye didn't have much to do with the hands-on of the business. Fun fact: her new best friend wasn't into horses. Once she made the connection — Faye was the daughter of Ed Taylor, a well-respected trainer who'd lost his life in a car accident earlier that same year, along with his wife and middle son — she knew Faye's trauma.

"I'm sorry about your family," she'd murmured, exchanging a cautious glance, catching a chink in the armour of this person she'd just met but already determined had barriers of her own. They became friends because of the mutual acknowledgement of the other's darkness. It was a stronger bond than shared music taste or movie star fandom or whatever forged friendships between teenage girls. Faye had never said much about her parents' and brother's passing, and likewise, Liv had never offered to share the story behind her own family's move to Ontario. It wasn't the details that mattered, somehow.

"Are you going to the sale?" Faye asked in an unusual change of topic. The Canadian Thoroughbred Yearling Sale was coming up at Woodbine.

"I'm helping Jake scope horses all weekend so I'll be around," Liv said. An important piece of information for a prospective yearling buyer was the anatomy of the young horse's throat. Horses that couldn't breathe properly understandably didn't make the best racehorses, so they were examined prior to auction with a diagnostic known as endoscopy. She completely expected to be exhausted and tired of adolescent Thoroughbreds after the next few days, but she'd learn a lot.

"Dean's looking at a bunch this weekend," Faye said of her older brother who'd taken over training duties after Ed Taylor's death. "I'm sure you'll see him around."

"Are you coming down at all?" Liv asked. Sale day was its own kind of social event for racetrackers, and despite Faye's aversion to horses, the social side attracted her.

"Hmm, not sure," Faye said, popping a cookie into her mouth. "I might still need to avoid what's-his-name. Plus, first day of school, right?"

"See?" Liv said. "I can't have any reason to avoid New Guy if he doesn't crash and burn on the working interview today, because he'll be living here. Awkward."

Faye brightened. "He's going to be living here? Oh, this just gets better and better." Her grin was wicked.

"No one needs that kind of complication."

Faye swung her legs to the side, resolutely planting sandaled feet on the patio, and drained the last of her spritzer. "Come on. Let's go check this man out." Then her phone rang, Faye looking decidedly irritated as she snatched it from the table and stared at the screen. She sighed. "Dean. Hang on."

Liv dragged her fingers through her nearly dry hair and pulled it into what was a messy ponytail by reality instead of design. Ratty pool hair could only look a mess. She prayed she'd just been, literally, saved by the bell.

Sure enough, Faye sighed again after hanging up. "I've got to go home. The computer is giving Dean grief. Why am I the only one who can sort these things out?"

Liv shrugged and suppressed a grin. "I'm sure there will be other opportunities for you to meet New Guy if he passes today."

"From what Emilie tells me, he should get advanced standing." Faye rose and rifled through her bag for her car keys.

It was a relief not to have to succumb to Faye's demands. She didn't imagine Nate Miller wanted to endure any more ogling than he might already have suffered today. It wasn't any more right to treat a guy like that than a woman, was it? Not that it was something she'd ever really thought about before he'd come along.

She saw Faye out and went upstairs to shower. With only a few days left before classes started, and those likely to be dominated by her responsibilities at the sale, she wanted to get on Claire today, because who knew how consistent she'd be once school began? She had to face the reality that if Nate Miller had indeed "passed" today — and she couldn't imagine he hadn't — he might have to complete Claire's education, no matter how much she hated the idea. School was going to come first, whether she wanted it to or not.

It was earlier than she wanted to ride, though. The staff would be bringing horses in and feeding. Finishing the day's routine. Which meant, as likely as not, Nate Miller would still be around. She both didn't want to seem like she was checking up on him and didn't want to feel like the owner's daughter, sweeping in after lounging by the pool, now coming to the barn to ride her horse. Not that he would know she'd been lounging by the pool. And she had been up since four, in at the track to help groom and gallop, assisted Jake, then done laps in said pool before her brief interlude with Faye. But he wouldn't know that, either. Still... she'd invited him for this working interview. Checking in was what she should do.

She timed it right, getting to the training barn just as they were gathering after the work was done, exchanging their last comments before they said their "see you tomorrows" or "have a good nights" and headed their separate ways. It looked as if the novelty had worn off for the regular staff, and Nate didn't appear traumatized, so that was a good sign. She suppressed a grin at that thought as she approached the group. *I'm sorry, I can't possibly work here. These women will not leave me alone.*

"How'd it go?" she asked, zeroing in on him.

"Good, I think. The girls whipped me into shape."

Did they have to giggle? She'd spoken too soon about the novelty, apparently.

"We've taken a vote." Kyrie, who had been around the longest, spoke. "If you don't hire him, we're all quitting."

Even she had to laugh, glancing at Geai. "You too?"

"I'm innocent of whatever those three are up to," he said. "But if that happens, you and Emmy can't go back to school because it will be up to the three of us to run this place."

It wasn't an endorsement — she'd grill Geai more on the day's details after everyone had gone — but, "It sounds like my hands are tied here. You have Geai's cell? Let him know when you want to move in."

CHAPTER ELEVEN

HE SET the guitar case next to the piano. The view out the big picture window grabbed him for a moment before he turned back toward the room. "Thanks for helping out."

"My pleasure," Emilie said. She sounded like she was sharing an inside joke with herself, standing next to the couch with the last box. "Where do you want this?"

"I don't know. Anywhere."

There hadn't been much stashed in the back of the Mustang, though it was probably more than he needed because he'd survived just fine on what he'd packed in his duffel bag. The only important things he hadn't dug out were his helmet and boots, both of them old and worn. A new helmet probably wouldn't be a bad idea — those things expired, apparently, and there was a good possibility of landing on his head, getting on yearlings — but he'd take those old worn boots over a shiny new pair any day. He loved those boots. They were part of him. He'd rue the day he'd have to replace them.

"Sorry I don't have much to offer by way of refreshment." He pulled a six-pack of Diet Pepsi from the bare-bones groceries he'd set on the counter. He wasn't a big pop drinker, but every now and then it hit the spot. Today — another muggy Ontario day spent lugging boxes up those stairs — was one of those times. He offered a can to Emilie. "Sorry. Warm cola is kind of gross."

She held up a finger and walked into the kitchen, opening a cupboard from which she extracted two plastic glasses. Then she peered into the freezer of the fridge, a white, no-name thing, and emerged with an ice tray, though she eyed it suspiciously.

"I'm not sure how long these have been here, but they haven't completely sublimated, so that's something, if you're game," she said.

"The acid in the Pepsi should overpower anything evil in them, right?"

"It's not as if ice goes bad," she agreed. "It just might pick up some undesirable flavours."

He slapped the counter lightly. "Hit me, then."

"It's too hot in here," she said as she cracked the ice tray, distributing the cubes between the two cups before pouring the Pepsi. She handed him one, the ice quickly melting as it bounced in the foam. "I opened the window earlier to air it out, but you might want to close it and turn that air conditioner on. We can sit downstairs."

The picnic table set on a strip of lawn near the barn was weathered to grey and had a character all its own. Even though the sun was starting to drop toward the treetops, the heat was holding. The shade was nice. A breeze would be better.

Nate sipped from the glass. He'd been right — the chemical-sweet of the aspartame masked any peculiar flavours the aged ice might have contributed. Ice which was long gone, leaving the cola just cool enough to be almost refreshing.

"So what's the deal? I don't like to make assumptions, but

I'm guessing you and your sister are both still in school?" It hadn't seemed appropriate for him to quiz Emilie during his tour, but she seemed to be open to friendship, at least. He liked that he could ask her anything, when Liv was a total closed book. Would that change over time? Who knew? To be fair, he'd already spent more time with Emilie than with Liv.

Emilie nodded. "I'm in first year Environmental Toxicology, and Liv is in third year vet school."

"Wow. A couple of smarty-pants, then." He grinned.

She rolled her eyes. "I saw your resumé. You have to have half a brain to take kinesiology."

"Only half, though."

She snorted. "You're not fooling me. Though I might question your sanity, leaving Alberta to come to Ontario. I'd love to go out there."

Ironic that it was wanting to preserve his sanity that had made him leave. "It's a nice place to visit," he said. The only thing he might miss about Calgary right now was the drier climate from the higher altitude.

Her expression made him think she was inputting it all into her computer of a mind — his words, his face, the minutiae of his body language — trying to decide what to push, what to leave alone.

He and Emilie both turned at the unmistakable sound of an approaching horse, soon accompanied by the sight of Liv on a small bay with lots of white hacking out alone. The length of the horse's tail, as well as the immature build, gave the animal away as a yearling, though the baby had a big walk for such a little thing, stepping out with confidence. Those legs were long. He'd bet that one was going to grow. Probably had a slow start for whatever reason — born early, maybe, because he couldn't imagine anything on this farm not being properly nourished.

She — because that feminine face had to belong to a filly — would catch up.

"That's Claire," Emilie said. "I'm not sure you're going to get anywhere close to that one."

The wry twist of the young woman's lips made him wonder if her meaning was two-fold. "Obviously she's been well-started already."

"Hey, Liv," Emilie called.

Liv turned her head, like she'd just seen them; smiled slightly and lifted a hand. Her gaze lingered on him, but she didn't add words to it. No, *get moved in all right?* Or *welcome to the crew.* Whatever. Claire wasn't the least bit worried about the two humans at the picnic table. She took them in with more interest and far less suspicion than her rider.

When he turned back to Emilie, she was watching him.

"Things to know," she began. "If you're silently watching my sister thinking she's all intriguing and you want to get to know her and maybe date her, just get that out of your head right now. She's not really that mysterious. It's pretty straight-forward, actually. She doesn't date."

"Did I ask?" He was partly amused, but a little insulted. He had no intention of putting the moves on Liv. He'd figured all that stuff out on his own.

"Just getting it out there, just in case."

"Got it," he said. "Now tell me something useful."

"Liv's best friend, Faye? Faye and her brother Dean have the farm just down the road, Northwest. Faye is pretty much Liv's opposite. If you ever meet her, you can be pretty sure she won't even wait for you to suggest anything. So if you're looking for something, there you go."

He chuckled. "Good to know."

"And if you're not? Just — hide, or something." She sipped

from the cup with a wave of her free hand. "You're on your own with the girls on the farm."

"I don't date either." Anymore. "So that solves that."

"A life less complicated?"

"Absolutely. What about you?"

"Who has time for that?" She proffered her glass, and he met it with his. He felt like he'd found an ally.

She touched the screen of her phone, checking on the time. "I have to go. I'll see you around when I come up for air from my study cave."

He took her empty plastic glass from her and stood. "Thanks for the intel."

She nodded at the cups. "There's a blue recycling bin in the feed room. Don't let me find those in the garbage."

"Are you sure they're recyclable?"

"Of course I'm sure. I bought them."

"Environmental tox. Got it." He grinned as she gave him a sideways smile and walked toward the house.

He was sorry he probably wouldn't see much of Emilie, but not seeing much of Liv seemed like a good thing. Sounded like if they avoided each other, they'd both be happy.

He dropped the cups in the blue box and made his way upstairs, the hollow sound of his running shoes on the wooden steps leaving him feeling lonely. In the apartment, the picture window drew him, a lookout that let him survey his new world. He could see Emilie strolling along the lane, then Liv and Claire returning, the two sisters probably exchanging words as they passed. Then Emilie disappeared from sight, leaving him watching horse and rider.

Together the two of them made a pretty image, the young woman and her mount. Liv Lachance with her picture-perfect life. Must be nice, that life. The fancy house, the white-fenced farm with its rolling hills inhabited by well-bred horses. The clear career path, the bankroll behind it. Home sweet home.

How long before it felt like home for him? Or was it just a step on the road? A halfway house for wayward boys. He wanted Liv's crystal-clear view of the future. He didn't care what it was; he just needed the security of knowing he had some kind of purpose.

Following them until the window's border ended the vignette, he turned to the piano, staring at it, then walked a wide circle around it to one of the boxes. He hadn't taken the time to label anything when he'd packed back in Calgary. It had been a rapid sorting of what to take, what to leave behind.

Inside was an odd assortment of photos, framed eight-by-tens he had to wonder why he'd bothered to bring along. But buried beneath them was a six-by-eight, and now it made sense. The others had only been there to hide this. Too bad he'd forgotten.

It was one of those stand-up frames, not the kind with a hook to hang on the wall. He forced himself to look at the shot. He had his arm around Cindy. His older brother Phil was on her other side, his younger brother Tim next to him — all of them slathered with mud from some adventure race; all of them with huge smiles. Even Tim, who was the shy one of the bunch; sweet like their mother, reserved like their father.

He rubbed the film of dust from the frame, then set it on top of the piano, not exactly sure why. A reminder? A torture device? A prompt to do better? But better at what, exactly?

He slid onto the bench and stared at the keys. He should get it tuned. Lifting one hand, then the other, his fingers hovered, like they no longer knew what to do, where to go — an extension of the rest of him.

CHAPTER TWELVE

Sweltering September heat and three days of showing made for compliant baby racehorses. Liv helped Jake with the last-minute scopes, holding the yearlings with the shank in one hand and twitch in the other. The first day there had been a lot more fight in some of them. Who could blame them? It was probably the first time most of them had experienced someone guiding a long tube up a nostril and into their throat. All Liv's soothing tones did little to pacify the ones who resisted. Today, horses and help alike were tired after three days of going in and out of stalls, walking up and down for viewings. The first day's sales barn drama, which typically involved someone getting loose from a handler, and possibly an ambulance for an injured worker, had settled into a more placid routine.

Sales day was busy for all involved. Buyers taking one last look at their favourites, consignors jumping at their demands, grooms putting the final spit and polish on the early numbers. The yearlings all literally had a number, affixed that morning, glued to their left hip that matched their pedigree page in the sales catalogue. Yes, glue. A total pain to get off.

Jake, with the box of the endoscope slung by a strap across his chest, slid the eyepiece toward Liv, holding it so she could view the upper airway of their most recent patient. He waited for Liv's assessment.

"Left laryngeal hemiplegia," she recited, recognizing a common dysfunction that affected the horse's breathing.

Jake nodded. Not good news for the seller; a potential deal for a buyer, though that savings would be used up by surgery to correct the issue.

"That's it for a while," Jake said as he stepped out of the stall, Liv releasing the horse. "Don't turn your phone off."

That was a vet's life, wasn't it?

There was always an air of anticipation when the day of the auction arrived, even if the Canadian Thoroughbred Horse Society wasn't on the same level as Keeneland September in Lexington, Kentucky, with its million dollar babies, which started next week. Past success stories graced the cover of the inch-thick softcover book listing the yearlings alphabetically by their mothers' names, this year starting with the letter M.

She'd long since drained her water bottle, but some of the consignors were handing them out for free, and she gladly accepted one. Emilie would have chastised her for contributing to plastic in the landfill, not having the foresight to bring enough refillable bottles with her. The water was cool, though, soothing her parched throat. She wished she could dump it over her head to wash away the layer of dust that had settled on her skin.

With a loud crackle, the public address system started up, and the announcer began his spiel, going over terms and conditions — the dry reading that filled the pages at the front of the catalogue. The walking area was filling up with people as the first yearlings made their way over. It was always busier here than in the actual pavilion where the seats were.

Liv glanced around and caught sight of a familiar form. Bent over at the waist as he leaned on the railing, Dean Taylor studied an open catalogue gripped in both hands, the tips of colourful sticky tabs jutting from its pages, designating horses he'd made notes on; maybe planned to bid on. Liv sidled up next to him. Even hunched as he was, the knee of one long leg popped so his left shoe rested on the ball of his foot, he was taller than her.

"Hey Dean," she said, pulling her own catalogue from the crook of her arm. "Why are you here so early?"

He glanced up and grinned with brown eyes just like Faye's, his dark unkempt hair falling over his brow, making him look boyish, though he was in his thirties. "Skipping school already? That's setting a dangerous precedent, isn't it?"

She grinned back. "I have a vet's note." She extracted her pen from where she'd jammed it between the pages and started absently drawing a line through the outs as the announcer listed the horses that had been withdrawn. "This is a justifiable absence. We never do anything important on the first day back, anyway."

She and Dean were far more similar than she and Faye. Maybe it was the oldest sibling thing. They were the serious ones. And Dean was a prime example of someone who had given up school for racing. She'd learned from Faye that training racehorses was what he'd really wanted to do; that he'd felt banished by his father, who'd insisted he get a proper education. The racing industry was far too fickle. But according to Faye, Dean was so much happier now, even though they'd had more than their share of rough patches with their farm. Sad, though, that it had taken death for him to have the chance to pursue his passion. Wasn't Dean a case in point for following her own?

Now that there were horses in the walking ring, the energy

level escalated. Those sleepy yearlings were waking up, confronted with yet more unfamiliar sights and sounds and smells: the crowd, the barbeque just outside cooking burgers and hot dogs, the buzz of the PA, the bid spotters in their elevated pedestal in the middle of it all.

Dean's eyes locked on the horse closest to them — hip number one — so Liv flipped quickly to the page to refresh her memory. She'd seen so many horses, and rarely had time to make notes, so there was nothing on this colt. But he piqued her interest because he was by Starway, Triple Stripe's own stallion.

Being first in the ring was not a good thing for a seller, because inevitably some potential buyers were late. While it looked busy in here, it wasn't as crowded as it would get. It gave a trainer like Dean — who didn't operate with the same budget the big names did — the chance to snag a bargain.

Physically, Liv could see why Dean liked this colt. Like Starway, he was dark bay, so dark his black points almost blended with the rest of him. A bright white spot popped from the middle of his forehead, big and feathered into his coat colour at the edges. He was well balanced and had a handsome head and a pleasant expression. He was alert, ears, eyes and nostrils all taking in the bustle, but he wasn't overly nervous. And he had a great walk, a sexy swing to his hips as his hind foot fell into the print of the corresponding front with a perfect cadence.

Even though it was extremely peoplely here — something that usually triggered her anxiety — she loved the atmosphere, the thrill of immersion in the possibility of it all. Another entry point to this sport she loved. Everyone was here to watch the horses, so she was free to observe unhindered. Dean was the perfect sales partner, because he was exactly the same. They fell into silence, watching the colt circle at the last stage before going into the ring. Then he was gone from their sight as the ring man led him through the doors.

The announcer extracted every highlight from the colt's pedigree as he talked the yearling up. Then finally, the auctioneer took over, and the rapid-fire ramble began. She and Dean shifted their eyes to the monitor that showed the view inside the pavilion.

The colt still held it together, though the small area in which the handler maneuvered him always seemed precarious to Liv. It was a raised platform in front of the auctioneer's stand, and all that separated it from the drop to the concrete floor and tiered seats of the pavilion were strands of rope. Thick rope, sure, and she'd never seen a yearling go through it; nevertheless her imagination could picture it and it always made her hold her breath, her heart in her throat, until the final SOLD! came.

The ring man walked the colt forward and turned him to present the other side. He stood, regally surveying his surroundings, an image that might inspire buyers to picture him posing in the winner's circle. The bidding was healthy; the numbers on the board displayed both in Canadian and American dollars, tripping upwards, four figures leaping to five.

It didn't really happen that you could inadvertently buy a horse at these things. People on the outside always worried or joked about that, afraid to twitch or scratch for fear of finding themselves with a horse they didn't intend to buy. There were too many checks and balances in place. She watched Dean from the corner of her vision. Sure it was subtle — a raise of a finger, a nod as he made eye contact with the bid spotter — but should he end up having the highest bid, he'd have to sign a slip, which a runner would take to the sales office. His credit would be verified. If the office found an error, they'd bring the yearling back into the ring and sell the horse again. Not even the underbidder was automatically on the hook.

Dean was all business now, poker face in place. The auctioneer's pitch had slowed. There was a rally back and forth, from one court to the other — someone in front was bidding against Dean here in the back, an intimate dialogue happening between the trainer and the spotter. Even though Liv knew all that stuff about inadvertent bidding, she kept herself still. The spotters knew who she was, the daughter of someone who had bought horses at this sale. She could be an agent. But as much as she liked this colt, she wasn't here to buy anything.

The next yearling waiting to go in the ring jumped when the auctioneer punctuated his final declaration. "Sold, to Steve in the back for twenty-two thousand." Steve was the bid spotter. Dean had got the colt.

"Congrats!" Liv said, patting him lightly on the back as her phone vibrated in the pocket of her jeans. She dragged it out and scanned the screen. Jake. "Gotta go."

"Hey — can you guys break this one for me?" Dean stopped her.

"Probably. I'll talk to Geai and get back to you."

She rushed off to meet Jake, frustration erasing the excitement of Dean's purchase. She'd love to start that colt, but she wasn't the one who would have that pleasure.

CHAPTER THIRTEEN

"Do we get to watch?" Trisha asked.

Nate caught the tone of his co-worker's comment, and it wasn't suggesting she was interested in the yearlings. He was getting used to their joking, but was it really this strange to have a guy working with horses around here? With riding horses, maybe, but racehorses? Al had always had mostly men working for him. Not that he was against women like some of the old-timers were; it's just the way it worked out, the demographics of it all. Thanks to Geai, Nate was just outnumbered three to two, but Geai only popped in and out throughout the day, leaving Nate to fend for himself most of the time. The manager was here now, at least as they gathered to bring the yearlings in so they could chill before the next stage of their lives began.

"I'm selling tickets," Nate said dryly. If he was going to stay here, there was only one thing to do: fight back. And by fight, he meant, give as good as he got.

"No," Geai said, with one word putting mock pouts on their faces. "After lunch, you'll finish the broodmare barn. And if you still have time after that, you can pick out the yearlings' fields."

Trisha, who was in her mid-twenties, sighed audibly, her dark red hair pulled away from her round face in a tight ponytail so there was no missing her expression. All of it didn't exactly make him uncomfortable, but at the track, the ratio would likely be more in his favour.

It was early days yet, but he liked the job so far. Regular farm chores were fine with him, and everyone pulled their weight. Turning out, bringing in. He liked mucking stalls; when the rest of them finally fell into silence, it let him think, and somehow the honest hard work left him more optimistic than he'd been in a long, long time. Same shit, different day, as the saying went, but there was nothing wrong with that.

He fed the horses breakfast, watered off and did night check on Geai's day off, and though he would have been happy to do it more often, the old man wouldn't let him. He was pretty sure "day off" for the manager only meant he avoided the help. None of them had ever been asked to do anything with the stallions. Maybe Liv or Emilie did that. But Nate gathered Liv went into Woodbine on weekends to gallop, and he wasn't sure of the extent of Emilie's involvement with the farm activities beyond social media convenor and tour guide. He'd have to ask, next time he saw her. She'd be back at school now, so he didn't know when that would be.

He was looking forward to starting the yearlings. They'd been out all night and had their grain reduced for a few days to encourage more willing attitudes for today's first lessons. They walked in agreeably enough and dove into the piles of hay in the stall corners.

"We'll grab the last two?" Nate turned to Kyrie as he secured a stall door.

One last yearling and the babysitter, a plump red off-track

Thoroughbred gelding named Twizzle, waited at the gate. By the look of the yearling's bleached chestnut coat and unkempt tail, the colt hadn't seen much of the inside of a stall in who knew how long. He was a complete contrast to the Triple Stripe homebreds, whose manes had been shortened, bridle paths cut. They'd been given some attention after being dragged in from the field, like kids with new haircuts for the first day of school.

The colt was a good size, but stood a safe distance from his companion, wary of the old gelding. Nate took a step toward him as Kyrie snapped her lead to Twizzle's halter, and the colt took a step backward. Nate stopped. This one was going to be fun. It didn't help that he couldn't use the older gelding as a buffer. He tipped his head to Kyrie, and she walked Twizzle toward the gate. Nate followed, and the colt, who had enough herd instinct not to want to be left out by himself, followed too. Nate slowly snapped on the rope.

"Hold up a sec, Kyrie."

She did, and the colt stopped and dropped his head, his nostrils vibrating with a quiet snuffle. He touched Nate's arm with his nose. Not completely feral, then. *Good.*

"All right. Let's see how this goes," Nate said.

Geai was waiting outside the training barn, arms crossed, well wide of the door. Twizzle disappeared into the darkness of the aisle. The colt got within ten feet, and stopped.

Geai stepped forward with a low, slow sweep of his arm, and that pressure was enough to move the colt. Another good sign all was not lost. The colt was just scared and hadn't been exposed to much, but with patience, patience, patience, maybe they'd get him broke sometime before his third birthday, Nate thought wryly.

Not that what he did resembled the vision that word might conjure for someone outside this sphere. Breaking, broke —

those words still got tossed around in the horse world, even if the only place you were likely to see bronc busting these days was at a rodeo. Gentling wasn't really accurate — he couldn't control what had happened before he met a horse, which meant sometimes there were ugly moments whether he liked it or not. For the rest of these — raised right — starting under saddle was a mere formality. This colt would be a challenge. He'd need to build trust. He couldn't afford any ugly.

"Just put him in the first stall on the left, there," Geai said, now that the colt was moving.

That suited Nate just fine, because he wasn't sure they were getting the yearling much farther into the belly of this whale. It took another wave of Geai's arms to encourage him into the stall. Nate wondered how loading on the trailer to get him here had gone.

The energy the colt gave off in the stall wasn't positive, and in the interest of safety, Nate left quickly.

"I won't be getting on that one anytime soon," he said, watching the colt spin.

"But I'm making popcorn," Kyrie quipped.

"Broodmare barn," Geai growled. "After lunch." Then he turned to Nate. "I'll meet you back here at one o'clock."

Nate nodded. He watched the colt for a while after Geai and Kyrie left. The colt stood still now, at least, but his eyes were wide as he returned Nate's gaze, his ears twitching forward and back. Nate felt called out, like the colt saw through him. He'd have to rediscover his own confidence to pass some along to this one.

He jogged back to the apartment, then changed into running clothes, throwing a handful of peppermints into a pocket. As he pushed buds into his ears, he cued up his designated playlist and set off.

It felt like he was the only human on the farm, the others

either taking off into town for lunch or staying in the cool of the break room to eat what they'd brought. There was no sign of anyone at the house, though there never was, the front of it facing the other way and the surrounding trees and fence providing privacy to the back. When he reached the stallion area, Geai was likely tucked away inside getting his own lunch. It was hot, so the stallions were inside. The shade of the wooded area as he dashed in gave him relief from that, sweat freely dripping from his pores.

He followed the path, watching his step for roots and rocks and the piles of manure Emilie had warned him about. He could feel the magic of the trees, their secrets and stories, but didn't slow until he emerged on the other side.

The girls were waiting for him. They gathered at the fence, ears pricked, eyes expectant.

"Hey, ladies! How are we today?"

These were the maiden mares and the older matrons who hadn't had a baby this season for whatever reason. All were in foal for next year. They would be the early group, with January and February due dates. The star, as Emilie had informed him the day of the interview, was a beautiful bright chestnut with a zig-zag of white starting above her eyes and tripping down the bridge of her nose, stopping short of her nostrils. Sotisse, Sovereign Award winner, carrying one of the first of Just Lucky's offspring. Next to her was Just A Cameo, dam of Just Lucky. She'd lost her foal this year, he'd heard, but had been bred to a big Kentucky stallion named Coincidence. She was a lovely bay, a few shades lighter than her successful son. Just Lucky had helped earn her Canadian Broodmare of the Year status the year he'd won the Triple Crown.

He doled out peppermints, then finished the run with a sprint and bounded up the stairs. Time for a quick shower and something to eat before he met Geai. In just a few days, he'd probably lost at least five pounds of the sloth weight he'd gained these past eight months of feeling sorry for himself. He didn't own a scale, though... and wasn't ready to buy one. It was enough to be sure — mostly — he could make race riding weight if that day happened to come.

Geai was already there, topping up waters, tossing more flakes of hay. When he finished, he waved Nate over and started putting names to faces.

"Don't worry about that one," Geai said as they passed the first stall. "That's Claire. No official name yet."

Nate recognized the bright white face that popped up. It was the filly he'd seen Liv on the day he'd moved in. "How come?" he asked, even though Emilie had already told him he wouldn't be working with Claire. "I don't mean the name."

"She's Livvy's project."

Nate realized he'd stopped, returning the filly's wall-eyed stare. That one didn't miss a trick. She felt like an old soul. He remembered how non-reactive she'd been that day. Liv had looked more worried than she had.

"What's the story there?" he ventured.

"Claude bought her at the November sale in Lexington last fall. He went down for a broodmare. The van that came from Kentucky had the broodmare on it, and this one, too. She's New York-bred. The stallion is okay, but the mare wasn't much. Got her for a song."

"Why, though? What's he going to do with a New York-bred?"

"He felt sorry for her. As you can see, she's not very big. Imagine her as a weanling — she was just little, and not in the best condition. Can't fault her conformation or attitude, though. He'll try her at the track. If she shows nothing there, Liv will make her a riding horse."

That was sweet. The girl had a pet.

He probably shouldn't call her a girl — it would probably offend her. Also, he should probably stop being so snarky. He broke away from his staring contest with the filly and followed Geai to the next stall.

"This is Just Gemma, a full sister to Just Lucky." There was obvious pride in the manager's voice, matched by clear affection for the filly as he slipped open the door and let her nuzzle his hand.

"Nice," Nate replied. The filly was a lighter bay that Just Lucky, her colour more like her mother Just A Cameo's, but her build was similar to her famous brother. High hopes for that one, he'd bet.

He tried to remember the names Geai rattled off — the official Jockey Club registered ones. Two colts next: Sans Défaut. Excursion. The truth was, if no one told him their barn handles, because they no doubt had them, he'd make up his own, anyway.

"The last three are boarders, just in for breaking. This one here should be okay. A colt bred just down the road. Friends of ours, Dean and Faye Taylor at Northwest Stud. They spend some time with theirs."

That name jarred his memory because of Emilie's warning about Faye Taylor. Who was Dean, again? The brother, he recalled.

In the next stall stood a tall, good-looking yearling, dark coat polished to a sheen, his halter brand new with a shiny brass plate. Nate hadn't seen him before, but the white square with its black number one explained that before Geai did.

"Also for Dean, but he bought this one out of the sale yesterday. He's by our stallion, Starway. And your friend here," Geai continued, stopping in front of the last stall, "we don't really know anything about. A friend of Dean's. One of his owners. A favour."

Ah. One of those deals, which never bode well. But Nate kept his mouth shut.

"Ours all tie. I expect the Northwest-bred one might as well. The sale horse is anyone's guess. This one I suspect does not."

The shy yearling circled to the back of his stall with a wary look in his eye and a worried flutter of his nostrils. Liv's statement at the interview came to mind: *we're not in a big hurry to get them going.* Good thing, that, because this one wasn't getting anywhere fast.

Introductions complete, Geai waved Nate toward the tack room. "Everything you need should be in here."

For the first day, that wasn't much. A bridle with a simple snaffle bit, from which he removed the reins. A shaped felt pad. A surcingle. A grooming kit.

"We have driving lines," Geai said.

"Will I need them?" He raised an eyebrow at the old man. Was Geai going to tell him how things were to be done?

"Up to you." Geai shrugged. "You're the boss."

"I am, am I? Why don't I completely believe that?" His lips twisted up on one side.

"You're the one getting on them. If you don't want to long-line, that's your call. Now, if it looks like a wild west show, I might have something to say."

You think I'm some kind of cowboy? But he kept the retort to himself. "Long-lining is fine," he said, checking his irritation. "I just don't find it necessary most of the time. If once we've put in sixty days, you don't agree, let me know, and we'll do it your way next year."

"You intend to be around next year?" There was that look again, the old man sizing him up.

"I guess that remains to be seen. But gotta think positive, right?" At the moment, he had nowhere else to go. He left the tack room, Geai following, and hung the surcingle and head-stall on a hook outside the first stall, setting down the pad and grooming tote. "Not going to do much with them today, anyway. I just want to see where their heads are at. We can start with yours."

Yours. They weren't his; at least, not yet. By the end of the program, he might be enough a part of the team to change that to *ours*.

They buzzed through the Triple Stripe homebreds quickly. He'd meant it when he said he wasn't doing much with them today. It was more about assessment; a little meet and greet. Seeing what they knew, what they didn't.

They were pretty good with their feet. Seemed happy enough to be groomed. Of course the colts tried to nip — year-ling colts were yearling colts. Each of them was chill enough he introduced the surcingle, Geai joining him in the stall; snap-ping a lead rope to the halter, unsnapping the wall tie.

Nate placed the pad on their backs first with no more reac-tion than a quiver of the skin, like they were trying to dislodge a fly. He set the surcingle on top, moved it around a bit. Then reached under, holding the long strap around their barrel to be sure no one lost their mind before buckling it and holding it in place because it wasn't yet secure. When the yearling didn't explode — he'd seen that; some of them took a while to accept the restriction of it — he snugged it up enough he trusted it to stay in place, then took over the rope shank, Geai leaving the stall while he circled the baby first one way, then the other, because some of them waited till they moved to take offence, and that's when the explosion came. Those bugs needed to be worked out before he took the next step. But all the Triple Stripe homebreds handled the first day without a hitch.

The Northwest colt was a little less polished. Mostly it was his feet he fussed about. He tied okay, except for the bitey thing. When Nate tightened the surcingle and asked him to move forward, he hopped a bit, then got over it. In a couple of days, he'd be up to speed. The sale horse was good, too. The final one, though...

The last yearling went immediately to the back of his stall as soon as they approached. Nate hadn't even opened the door yet. When he slid it open, the colt spun his butt, putting his nose in the corner. Nate stopped and glanced at Geai.

"I guess this one's going to take a bit longer," Nate said. "Leave it with me."

Geai only gave a slight twitch of one eyebrow — more a gesture of speculation than doubt — then nodded.

"Be safe," was all he said.

"I've got worker's comp, right?" Nate grinned, and Geai laughed.

He didn't assume someone had mistreated the colt. It was possible, of course, but it was just as possible he'd simply not been handled, and was naturally suspicious. Just like people, some horses were extroverts, some were introverts, and you had to work a little harder to make friends.

I shall call you Arthur, he thought, watching the colt cautiously turn back to face the door after he'd closed it and stepped away. "Guess that's it for today then," he said to Geai, gathering everything up to return to the tack room.

"The girls would have been disappointed," Geai said wryly.

Nate laughed. "Maybe they saved a couple of stalls for me." At the very least, he'd be able to help them bring in.

Geai didn't rush off, waiting in the aisle with his usual arms-crossed posture until Nate reemerged. "You should go into Woodbine one morning and get licensed," he said. "Get on a couple. Let Roger see you."

"You haven't even seen me on a horse yet," Nate quipped. "Trying to get rid of me already?"

"I don't believe in holding people back."

Hmm. So the only person around here who was going to do that was him. This outfit was already proving to be a good place to work. It was all class, and he expected the track contingent was no different. Roger Cloutier, Claude Lachance's private trainer, might need a rider to go south. It'd be nice to spend the winter in Florida, wouldn't it? Expand his horizons. But...

"Thanks," he said. "That would be great. But not sure you'll chase me away that easily quite yet."

CHAPTER FOURTEEN

A SMATTERING of framed pictures rested on top of the buffet in neat black frames. Her parents' wedding photo; baby pictures of her and Emilie; high school graduation photos. There were no photographs of her extended family in the house, not even in the carefully curated album her mother had organized. It had been so long since she'd seen any of them, she wondered if she'd even recognize them now. Except for her grandfather. She was sure she would always recognize him.

Family meals were always more comfortable with Geai present, and he usually joined them at least once a week. It was his attendance that made the holidays bearable, though Christmas was really the only one that included unavoidable traditions. Easter and Thanksgiving celebrations were usually worked in around the track schedule, because what was a day off for most workplaces was an extra day of racing at Woodbine.

Her mother was an excellent cook — just another thing Liv was not. Liv could make a salad, or a grilled cheese, or fry an egg, but that was about it. She would never starve, but gourmet would never be her thing. She helped bring the food to the table — she could do that much — then sat next to her father as he poured wine for everyone but her. She didn't like it, or alcohol in general.

"How is Claire coming, Liv?" Her father turned his attention to her.

Claude Lachance had never been one to tell her she was pretty. Sometimes he would tell her she was smart. They were both more comfortable with this type of discussion. They could talk horses all day like old friends. Leave the personal out. They understood each other; that was all that mattered.

"She's doing well. Nothing phases her. I've even jogged her on the track a little."

"Are you sure you have time for her, with school?" her mother asked. There was a note of pride in her voice, because hard work was to be lauded. Taking on such a heavy course load was a badge of honour; handling it so well, another one, but heaven forbid anything else interfere with obtaining that lofty degree.

"Yes." She responded quickly, but didn't think she snapped. When she flipped her eyes to Geai, he was suppressing a grin.

"How's the new fellow?" Her father asked Geai.

"So far I'm impressed," Geai answered. "He's quiet and nononsense. The horses like him." If the horses liked you, chances were, Geai would too.

"I'm sure he'd be quite all right with Claire. Especially as she's so tractable," her mother inserted.

Liv's jaw tightened, teeth grinding. "I can manage, Maman."

"You should come watch him, Livvy," Geai said.

Now she shot him a look. *Whose side are you on, anyway?*

But, she should keep tabs on her selection for the position.

She'd let her schedule swallow her up; let Geai assume the duties that had always been his. She couldn't use that as an excuse. When she became a vet, she'd have to juggle all the things — clients, cases, finances, as well as her responsibilities at the farm — and somehow still find time for riding and working out, because both were crucial to her sanity. Veterinarians had one of the highest suicide rates of all professions. Compassion fatigue was real. They'd already discussed *well-being* in one of her courses this semester — social, occupational — and *resiliency* was becoming a theme. She had to manage it all.

"Maybe on the weekend," she said. "I should be home from the track before you start."

She didn't miss the way her mother's lips pressed together. The only reason Anne Lachance kept quiet about her galloping on the weekends was because after she was done, she helped Jake on his rounds. Liv would never understand how a horse-crazy teenager could give it all up when she met a man and got married. But her mother had. Didn't she miss it?

She'd seen photos of her mother riding. Galloping, even. But she'd never actually seen her mother on a horse in real life. Her father had always been the one to drop her off at her grandfather's farm; always the one to come to her shows. Never her mother. Anne had tolerated her daughters' involvement with horses only because it seemed unavoidable with her grandfather being who he was: an Olympic-calibre show jumper, though he'd never quite made it to the Games.

"I suggested he go in and get licensed at the track," Geai said.

Liv had to stop her mouth from falling open, her teeth indenting her bottom lip to be sure it remained closed. Why hadn't Geai told her first? Maybe it served her right, for dropping the ball on the follow-up.

"I hire him, and now you're sending him away?" She did

her best to look amused instead of irritated. "Do you want to encourage him to leave?"

"I want to show him we have trust he'll stay."

It seemed a little like leaving the cage door open so a bird had freedom to fly away.

"We won't be able to keep him on the farm forever," Geai said.

"Can't we?" Emilie said, her pleading tone balanced by a grin. Her mother smiled at that. Anne Lachance hadn't even met Nate Miller, and she probably liked him too.

"If you love something, set it free," Liv quipped. Emilie kicked her under the table. Liv turned to Geai with a slight tilt of her head. "You realize if he bails on us that I'll have to quit school and do the yearlings myself. It's too late to find someone else now."

She almost felt guilty for the way her mother's face twitched — but not quite.

Geai didn't seem concerned, whereas Liv thought it was a real possibility that helping Nate get his license was just facilitating his departure. Roger didn't need any exercise riders. With Liv, and sometimes Emilie, helping on the weekends, there was ample opportunity for the one he employed to have time off. They only had eight horses at the track right now. If Nate Miller had his license to gallop, what was stopping him from using it to find a job with someone else, or to start freelancing? There never seemed to be enough good freelancers. What Geai had suggested was giving Nate a free pass to leave. But there was some merit in presenting a test. If he stayed despite that, it would suggest a certain loyalty that was rare in this business. And the offer showed a kind of respect on Geai's part, didn't it? It acknowledged Nate had a choice. He didn't have to be here, helping them. A choice Liv envied. A choice she didn't have.

It wasn't as if she'd actually get to quit school and do the yearlings herself. Her mother would make sure of that. Her father would send them to another farm, one of the places around that offered that service for those who didn't have the personnel to do it themselves.

For that reason, Liv wanted Nate Miller to stay. Because even if she was still working with Claire herself, it would be far too easy to have the filly sent along with the others, if it came to that. Her mother would undoubtedly persuade her father on that point, and Geai wouldn't have much of a case against it, if he was even on Liv's side.

She helped clean up after dinner, then bolted to the training barn. There was just enough daylight left to end her hectic week on the perfect note.

Finding the barn gloriously deserted, save for the equine occupants, Claire's low nicker greeted her; grounded her. The performance of being a human this week left her exhausted. She needed this much easier connection.

She tacked Claire up quickly, covering the filly's frosted front legs with white polo bandages before slipping on the bridle. Claire mouthed the bit, curling her head around to Liv as Liv fastened her helmet before leading the filly out of the stall.

"Want a leg up?"

She nearly jumped out of her skin at the figure in the middle of the aisle. Nate. Where had he come from? Not that it was any surprise. When she was with the filly, Claire was her world. Her refuge; her port in the storm. She blocked out every-thing else.

Her response didn't come out right away. It wasn't even a case of the words being stuck in her brain; they didn't even form.

She didn't need his help. She'd gotten Claire used to the

mounting block so she wouldn't have to rely on someone being around for her to ride. Once her mind began to function again, she almost said, "What are you doing here?" But she quelled her natural response to this intrusion.

"Okay. Sure. Thanks." So maybe those lectures on emotional IQ had yet to sharpen the brain-to-voice signal. Did his lips twist? Humour well in those eyes?

Eyes that were very blue, she was reminded, when he was near enough to hold Claire's head. It was part terror, part thrill, his being so close. It brought up everything in her that was awkward and damaged. She blocked it out, buried it back where it belonged, and cocked her leg for him to wrap his hand around her ankle. Claire stood like an angel, oblivious to Liv's consternation.

"You could probably hop on her without my help," he said once she was up.

"True enough," she answered. Why hadn't she mentioned she didn't really need help? Maybe there was hope for the girl in her. Maybe one day, a guy — a guy like him — would round off her edges, temper her defences, help her trust. Make her believe. *Right.*

"What are you doing here, anyway?" she did finally ask, hoping she didn't sound suspicious, like he shouldn't be here. She wasn't sure he should be, though. She tucked her feet in the irons, adjusting them after she knotted her reins, because someone — him, it had to be — had changed the length of the stirrup leathers.

"I offered to water off when Geai said he was going to your place for dinner. And I thought I might play with Arthur."

Before she had a chance to say *that was nice of you* to the part about Geai, like a normal human being would, the second part of his answer stumped her. "Arthur?"

He grinned at her perplexed look, those perfect teeth of his making an appearance. "That shy colt. The one who's afraid of his own shadow?"

"Arthur?" she repeated, with *why* instead of *who* attached this time. Claire dropped her head, ears flopped to the side like an old track pony as she waited for Liv to process. If that was the case, they might be here a while.

"Arthur Dent?" Nate said. "In the immortal words of *The Hitchhiker's Guide to the Galaxy*: don't panic."

Liv grinned. "No wonder you get along with my sister. That's her favourite book."

He grinned back. "I knew there had to be a reason."

"I thought maybe Arthur Pendragon. Like you're trying to instill bravery in him."

"That might be a better idea," he said.

"How's he doing?" she asked, grateful for a topic that let her seem normal.

"He's a work in progress. You said no hurry, right?"

"Exactly right. Good luck."

"Thanks." His grin got a little crooked, then he turned back toward the barn.

"Thank you," she called after him, finally remembering her manners. Speaking of being a work in progress. "For the leg up."

He nodded, still smiling. A squeeze of her calves, and Claire stepped out. Just a walkabout tonight. No hurry.

CHAPTER FIFTEEN

EMILIE HAD INFORMED him there was a laundromat in town, and he'd driven by it on his way to Lucy's. He hadn't been able to resist going back for those butter tarts. He'd also noticed, however, there was a washer and dryer in the training barn. Weighing the pros and cons of driving into town versus horse hair on his clothes, he opted for the latter. He spent much of his time covered in horse hair anyway, so what difference did it make? Maybe hand-washing underwear would be a plan, though. He jammed jeans and t-shirts and socks and running shorts into a backpack; sniffed a sweatshirt he'd only needed a few times so far and tossed it back on his bed. It could wait.

The farm was quiet, the horses outdoors bathed by the early evening light, grazing in clusters, tails swishing at flies. He wondered how long it would be before the weather changed, late summer giving way to early fall, the evenings becoming cooler. Waking up to frost instead of dew as the sun rose.

He flipped on the tack room light. There were even detergent. *Sweet.* He started the first load, then peeked into the dryer. It was full of polo bandages, saddle towels and girth covers. He started singing "Another Saturday Night" as he rolled and folded. Except while he didn't have somebody, he didn't want somebody. Not now. Maybe not ever.

He'd just got to the part about arriving in town when he looked up and saw Liv standing in the doorway. He stopped abruptly, his mouth half open, mid-stanza.

Her eyes went from the horse laundry, to his laundry, to his face. Once he recovered, he almost said, *we have to stop meeting like this.* Two days in a row. But he didn't think they were quite there yet.

"Okay," she said, the slight quiver of a laugh in her voice. "If you decide to stay, I'll ask my father about getting something for your apartment."

If. It was like she questioned his commitment. Fair. He questioned it himself, and racetrackers were a notoriously transient bunch.

He watched as she picked a saddle cloth, girth cover and polos from his folded pile before collecting tack and a grooming kit. He didn't have to ask what she was doing and didn't think she wanted his help. She didn't really need him to leg her up, but last night it had felt polite to ask, and she'd been too polite to refuse. Should he offer again? Would it be too much? She probably just wanted to be alone. He got that. He was becoming a recluse himself. Was that bad?

He peeked around the corner, seeing her set it all outside Claire's stall and, grabbing one of the rope shanks hanging at the end of the barn, she disappeared.

It wasn't long before he heard the light clip-clop of Claire's unshod hooves on the barn aisle as Liv led her to her stall, but he stayed where he was and started sorting tack as he waited for the washing machine to finish. There wasn't a lot of dirty equipment, but he didn't clean it each day after working with the yearlings, so he was catching up. He decided it was best just to hide in here. If Liv wanted him, she could ask.

She didn't, apparently. The clip-clop came again, retreating this time until it became nothing. He went back to singing.

Once the first load was in the dryer, he decided it was a good time to play with Arthur. Pendragon was a better angle; perhaps auto suggestion could help the colt's confidence. Was that what Liv liked to read when she wasn't buried in a veterinary text? Which must be all the time, these days.

The colt's pasture mates shunned him, including the field's referee, the old gelding, Twizzle. Some babysitter. At least Arthur was easier to catch now, so that was a bonus. Coming in each day had helped, but it was tricky getting him out when the others wanted to swarm the gate. Nate distributed the flakes of tasty second cut hay he'd brought with him as a distraction and left them bickering over which pile was choice as he and Arthur slipped out.

It didn't take a rocket scientist to figure out the colt was claustrophobic. He obviously hadn't spent much time in a stall, and found the confinement stressful. Simple solution: Nate was building Arthur's trust outside. It was actually going better than expected. He didn't bother to lead the colt into the barn, instead going directly to the round pen where he'd left a hoof pick, set of brushes and a longe line.

Holding the end of the lead rope, he started currying Arthur in the middle of the pen. It was hard at this age — most babies hadn't learned to like peppermints and carrots, and apples were even more of an acquired taste. But Arthur seemed to enjoy the circular motion and itch relief of the rubber comb, so it became Nate's currency. The colt's coat was starting to darken and shine as the bleached hairs sloughed away. And maybe Liv didn't appreciate his singing, but the colt did, though it probably had more to do with the way it evened out his own heart rate and breathing than Arthur liking his voice or chosen playlist.

Arthur followed at his elbow when he returned the grooming kit to the other side of the fence and replaced the rope shank with the long, flat, cotton line. A flip of the end was all he needed to get the colt circling. A whip would have destroyed everything Nate had built. After a few turns at the walk, he moved the colt up to a trot with a flick and a cluck.

"Such a good boy," he crooned as Arthur jogged, the colt stretching his neck down, his nose at the same level as his knees. When he'd first met the colt, he never would have imagined they'd get this far in five days. No matter he'd bellied and backed the others in the stall and they were all ready for their first little rides outside. "So proud."

He hoped the colt's owner was a patient person.

It was dim by the time he returned Arthur to his non-friends. Tomorrow was Geai's day off, so Nate would hay and water once he'd folded the load of laundry in the dryer and started the next one.

Liv wasn't back yet. That filly of hers made him think. He might need them, for Arthur, as company; a lead. Obviously Twizzle would be useless in that capacity because Arthur was afraid of him. That went for the other colts as well. Normally he wouldn't think of pairing a filly and colt at this age, but Arthur hadn't shown even a hint of being studdish.

Claire would be good for it. She was completely non-threatening. The shy colt was a ways away from being ready for that, though. He kind of needed to get on the yearling before then. But there was no rushing the relationship. A jab in his side reminded him how that had gone with his ex. At the time he hadn't thought he'd been rushing, but looking at it now he might be ready to admit he had been.

Liv would be good for him, too. Not in a romantic way. She

was good for his ego, which somehow still existed after what had happened with Cindy. Because while it was fine for him to go out with Will to a club on his birthday and push away a fawning girl, and it was fine to flirt with Emilie and josh with the farm staff, it bothered him, apparently, that this girl — this woman — cared not one bit for him. He was an employee, that was all. And that was all he needed to be right now.

CHAPTER SIXTEEN

HER STUDY NOTES were words and sketches; not that she could draw very well. Like any horse-crazy kid, she'd doodled in the margins of her schoolbooks, but she'd never become adept. Funny that now such sketches were part of her schooling, rather than a distraction from it.

Not that she really needed to study equine anatomy. She knew the proper names as well as the lay names. She'd be able to speak to trainers, translating them as easily as her brain now translated French to English and back again. In track speak, the fetlock joint was the ankle, even though it really wasn't. The carpus was the knee, when the corresponding joint on the human body was the wrist. The tuber coxae was the point of hip. Trainers weren't going to magically start using scientific names. They didn't have much use for science at all. It was up to the vets to take the science and make it palatable.

No, she wouldn't be illustrating any anatomy texts, but the parts were where they were supposed to be, at least, even if the shapes weren't quite right. She picked another species on which to focus, comparative anatomy from first year undergrad

Biology the starting point on which to expand everything she needed to store in her memory. Medical students didn't know how easy they had it, with only one species to worry about, though having to deal with human patients might even things out.

A warm breeze fluttered the edge of the notebook pages, and she planted a hand on top of them to settle them, glancing up at the sky. Still clear, blue and cloudless above her, but the wind was picking up. It was almost time to pack up anyway, Geai emerging from the barn with a stud shank in his hands. She could study more tonight.

Just Lucky paced back and forth. The young stallion always had to be first. He pushed his head over the gate and Geai poked him in the muzzle every time he tried to nip. Liv didn't know how Geai kept up with it, because it was a constant natter, natter, natter. It made her laugh, because Geai said she let horses get away with stuff. Just Lucky was like a grandchild to the old farm manager, as much as Liv and Emilie were.

Lucky finally stopped his pestering and allowed the manager to loop the long chain part of the lead shank over the horse's nose, wrapping it around the leather of the noseband, then back under his jaw. From there, Lucky was relatively civilized, prancing lightly on the way to the barn. He hadn't covered a mare since the end of June, but he was still hopeful.

Just Lucky's first foal was due the third week of January, carried by Sotisse, her father's favourite mare. The mating combined the genes of the farm's two most successful runners. It was hard not to be excited about that one.

The foal could be nothing, of course. You could plan all you wanted — breed the best to the best — and still end up with a lot of disappointment. Lucky's success as a racehorse still seemed like a crazy, amazing dream. Claude Lachance's first-generation homebred. He'd purchased Sotisse because of her fashionable bloodlines with the expectation she would be an asset to his fledgling broodmare band — a gamble he'd thrown a lot of money at. A gamble that had paid off when she'd turned out to be a talented runner as well. Lucky was more a rags to riches story.

By rights, they should have bred Sotisse to a fancy, established, Kentucky stallion after her success at the track. She was worthy of such a match. The decision to keep her home, to breed to their own stallion in his first year standing stud, was not one that followed the rules. It wasn't about wise investment or common sense. It was about one thing and one thing only. A gut feeling. A dream. And while Liv was usually sensible to a fault, preferring to stick to the rules, on this one, she sided with her father. Her gut felt it, too. This foal would be special.

Geai and Lucky disappeared into the barn, Starway meandering over to the gate, content to wait while Geai attended to his demanding stablemate. Movement to the right pulled Liv's gaze away from the stallion. Nate, emerging from the woods.

He didn't look in her direction immediately, and she let herself watch him. She knew human anatomy too; once again allowed herself to observe his rather correct conformation. He wasn't a bad mover, either. She suppressed a smile, even though there was no one around to see it, then blushed when he looked over, though he was probably too far away to notice.

He stuttered a step, like seeing her had knocked him off stride. Then he lifted a hand and kept running, his eyes returning to his chosen course. The two of them were merely ships that passed, but hiring him had been the right call. It seemed to be working out. No one had anything negative to say about him. He kept to himself, much to the chagrin of the female staff, she was sure. Emilie seemed to have befriended him.

The real test would be what he did when the yearlings

finished with their sixty days. Would he stay? Or would he make his way to the track, hoping to find a winter job somewhere warmer? Especially if their trainer at Woodbine signed his application for an exercise rider's license. She wouldn't stay up here in the cold if she had the choice, so she could hardly blame him.

He waved and nodded at Geai too as the manager came out of the stallion barn, but didn't stop for Geai, either. As Geai brought in Starway, Liv extracted herself from the picnic table, threw her bag over her shoulder, and walked into the stable.

She could hear Lucky's feed tub rattling as he devoured his afternoon meal. *Clatter, clatter, thump.* Starway's hooves clomped on the brushed concrete aisle. Liv could just catch the wisp of his long, full tail sweeping behind him, swinging with the rolling of his massive hindquarters.

When Geai came out of the stall, Starway's tub now rattling in concert with Just Lucky's, Liv was watching the smaller stallion. He'd been popular this season with breeders, the new kid on the block in Ontario. There hadn't been a Canadian Triple Crown winner standing at stud in twenty years and the last one hadn't rocked the breeding world the way everyone might have hoped. That was the fun of this game. Lucky could just as easily turn out to be another mediocre stallion who might be better off removed from the gene pool.

Geai re-buckled the heavy leather halter he'd removed from Starway and hung it on a hook on the door.

"Isn't it your day off?" she chastised.

He ignored her like he always did. It wasn't that he didn't trust anyone else to handle the stallions, he just didn't trust anyone else to handle the stallions. Except maybe her. She suspected Nate would be capable of it too, though Geai would have to accept the idea first.

"Hungry?" he said instead.

"I ate something."

"Fruit? Bird seed?"

She ignored his teasing. He always complained she didn't eat enough. *Maybe that's why I'd be able to make weight without much effort and you outgrew your riding career in your early twenties,* she thought wryly. Such a shame he hadn't been blessed with that envious combination of structure and metabolism. Such a shame while she had, she might never have the chance to make use of it.

"I brought you vegetables," she said.

"I need a sandwich."

"You can put vegetables on a sandwich."

Geai rolled his eyes.

Napoleon greeted them at the door of Geai's cottage, his stocky black body swaying as his tail wagged. Liv had to wait her turn to greet the old Labrador, but took her time to lavish some love on him once Geai went on to the kitchen.

She didn't have to see what he was making to know what it was — Montreal smoked meat on rye. She reached into the sack of veggies she'd brought and pulled out a baggie of sliced carrots, pausing with her fingers on the fridge door handle.

"Would it kill you to put a piece of lettuce on that? It would balance the mutagens a little, at least."

"Lettuce doesn't go with smoked meat," he grumbled.

She sighed and tossed Napoleon a carrot stick, which he snapped from the air. The old dog might have slowed down in other ways, but not when it came to food. At least he'd share the veggies. It might feel like she was joking with Geai, these exchanges about his diet, but she worried about him. Had, since he'd lost his wife four years ago. She pulled out a textbook and nibbled on the carrots, sharing them with Napoleon while Geai ate.

Liv tucked her book back into her bag when he took his empty plate to the sink and cleaned it. He turned to face her.

"Ready to go?"

She nodded, pushing up from the table. Napoleon rose from where he'd stationed himself at her feet.

"Sorry, Napoleon. Dog-proofing isn't part of the yearling's training."

She felt like an outsider on her own farm, relegated to the sidelines. Nate Miller, doing the job she'd had to let go of. Geai held the bay filly — Gemma, a full sister to Just Lucky — and Nate went about checking the girth to make sure it was snug, popping down the stirrup irons with a slap of the leathers, running fingers over buckles on the bridle and adjusting keepers, checking the fit of the bit so it rested properly in the filly's mouth. Liv had no doubt he'd put it all on himself, so all this was a formality, but she appreciated his thoroughness.

He gathered the reins, already knotted to shorten them to a safe working length, and with no words passing between him and Geai, bounced from Geai's leg up and lowered himself into the saddle. His care and effortless athleticism stirred something in her she couldn't suppress, and it irked her. Good-looking guys made her nervous, sure. They didn't do *that*.

She focused on the emotions instead. Jealousy that Nate and Geai seemed to have the same ease of working together that she'd thought was special between her and the farm manager. Resentment, that she was stuck watching. Maybe it would all deteriorate from here and those first impressions would fall by the wayside to reveal, well... flaws in Nate Miller. It wasn't fair that he was both good-looking and competent.

Geai walked the filly forward, taking yearling and rider for an incomplete figure-eight in the small sand ring so that when Nate nodded and Geai turned them loose, they were travelling to the left. Before Gemma had a chance to think for herself, Nate gave a trill of chirps with his tongue and quick bumps with the inside of his heels and Gemma popped into an unsure trot.

From there, the way Nate kept her going seemed invisible, but his hands remained forward, giving her head complete freedom while his legs hugged her barrel, that pressure enough Gemma didn't consider slowing. After the first few strides he posted, tidy as any equitation rider, his body so controlled he didn't interfere with the yearling's precarious balance. Gemma's ears flickered like the antennae of an insect, gleaning information from his body, his constant presence commanding her attention so that her surroundings were inconsequential.

He continued with the pattern Geai had first led them through, changing direction across the diagonal, his weight and an open rein providing guidance. Doing so taught Gemma to steer, the filly no worse for not having spent a few days ground driving. Liv almost smacked her forehead with her palm. Such an intuitive way to do it. She glanced at Geai, who was watching her, and pursed her lips. Had the old man learned something too?

She'd been so engrossed she hadn't noticed anyone approaching until he was resting his arms on the top rail of the fence next to her.

"Hey, kiddo." Dean nudged her with his elbow as she glanced over. "Oops."

Liv's smile was interrupted as she returned her gaze to the ring, but she saw nothing awry. "What?"

"Baby had a little spook. All good now."

From Liv's perspective it appeared as if nothing had

happened, Nate carrying on at a now-lively jog, Gemma's focus all on him.

"He's good, eh?" Dean said. "He's got panache."

"Panache?" Liv smothered a laugh.

"Sure. What word would you use?"

"Not that one."

Nate was confident on a horse, definitely. More so on than off of one. But who was she to talk? He was somehow both still and animated up there, his subtle signals to his mount as clear as telepathy. She hated him a little more.

"I don't recognize him," Dean said. "Who does he gallop for in the morning?"

How have you not heard? Liv almost responded. But Faye wasn't likely to pass on the news of Triple Stripe's live-in help to her brother, when the main point of interest for Faye was Emilie's report on the new guy's hotness factor.

"No one."

"So I can steal him away, then?"

"Absolutely not." It reminded Liv again of Geai's comment about getting Nate licensed. If he was as good on a racehorse as he was with the babies, someone at Woodbine would snap him up so quick they'd be back to square one here on the farm, trying to find another staff member. Maybe he sucked at galloping. It was possible.

It was only a short session; just a few minutes both ways before he let Gemma walk. The bay filly was tired, though it was likely more from the brain work than the physical effort. Thinking was hard when you were a baby horse who had, to this point, existed with few expectations other than leading in and out from the pasture to the barn and back and picking up her feet politely for the farrier. Nate pointed Gemma toward the audience at the rail. He swung off and ran up his stirrups.

"She's a good girl," he said, scrubbing her withers with his fingernails before loosening the girth a hole. He eyed Dean, waiting.

Liv straightened. "Sorry. Nate, this is Dean Taylor, our neighbour."

The two men exchanged handshakes and polite smiles through the fence before Geai opened the gate, offering Nate the rope shank.

"I'll get your homebred next then, Dean," Nate said. All the charisma Liv had felt when he'd been riding seemed to seep away now that he was back on the ground. Her earlier feelings of resentment were replaced with ones of kinship. Maybe they were a little alike, she and this guy.

She followed off to the side, absently listening to Nate and Dean talk. She wanted to hop on one of the yearlings herself and see if she could replicate what he'd done. If she wasn't feeling so out of sorts, she'd have suggested it — even though she had studying to get back to. It would be rude to leave now that Dean had arrived, so she had an excuse to stay and watch some more.

"How's the other colt coming along?" Dean asked.

"Arthur?" Nate said.

Dean looked at him blankly.

"That's what Nate's calling him," Liv interjected. "Though there's some debate whether he's supposed to be a knight or a displaced human on a very strange intergalactic voyage."

Nate slid a glance her way and grinned. "He's coming along. I might do a bit of long-lining with him, though. The whole 'get on and go' thing probably wouldn't go over so well with him. The driving lines will get him used to something moving on his sides so he maybe doesn't drop me on my head when I'm finally on him."

She arched her eyebrows, though he wasn't looking at her, his gaze focused somewhere on the ground about six feet in front of him, from what she could tell. So, he wasn't rigid in his methods. Whatever was best for the horse. Couldn't she find some objective reason not to like him?

She stayed long enough to help turn the yearlings back out. Dean had wanted to watch Nate work with Arthur, and Liv couldn't resist the temptation to do the same. Today's baby step with the colt was the introduction to a surcingle and pad, which Liv thought the colt accepted surprisingly well. Dean continued to be impressed.

Dean went home. Nate went back to his apartment. Geai lingered.

"Why do you think he'd leave?" Geai asked.

"Because I probably would, in the same position. If I had the freedom to do so."

"You do, if that's really what you want."

"No. I don't," she insisted.

"So you would abandon me?" He didn't hide his broad grin.

"It's not as if you listen to me when I nag about your health, so..." She smiled back. "I'd better get back to studying."

She returned to the house, glancing up at the apartment as she passed it. She'd let the dust settle — in her mind — before getting on Claire.

CHAPTER SEVENTEEN

He reached Woodbine at quarter to eight, wishing he could skip this step — trudging into the trailer by the security entrance and announcing himself to the guard behind the counter.

The guard nodded and broadcast through the public address system, "Roger Cloutier, party waiting at the East Gate."

He squirmed. Not Nate's idea of a party, but then again, parties weren't really his thing. He should have texted when he'd arrived, but that would have meant Liv, because he didn't have the trainer's number. He'd never texted her before; they only communicated when they randomly ran into each other on the farm and then words were sparse. The guard could have called Roger directly, couldn't he? They must have the trainers' numbers on file. Maybe he was making a point of embarrassing Nate, or maybe he was just lazy.

A phone rang in short order, and the guard picked up a landline. Nate watched as he nodded.

"Okay. Thanks, Jo." He gathered a couple of forms and

pushed them to Nate on top of the counter. "Fill these out and I'll get you a guest pass."

Nate accepted the pen he was offered and scanned the documents before filling them out and sliding them back over the counter. Then the guard took his picture, sent him to an adjacent small office where a woman behind a desk smiled, took the access form and did her thing. The guard handed Nate a small piece of thermal print paper with a bar code and his photo on it when he returned. They took security seriously around here.

"You're good to go."

"Thanks," Nate said, stepping towards the door. "Oh — what barn are they in again?"

"Five. It's the second one facing the main track. But you'll have to park either at the kitchen or across from Barn Two. Six of one, half a dozen of the other, which is closer."

He left the trailer, tramping down the steps to the small lot beside it where he'd left the Mustang. He climbed behind the wheel and drove up to the shack, then handed his slip of paper to the guard. The guard scanned it, nodded, and opened the barrier.

Google Maps was his friend — he'd checked the layout of the Woodbine backstretch so he could make a good guess where the kitchen was, and followed the network of paved roads between the barns, cutting behind the first row of them because the direct route was blocked off during training hours. The dusty old car with its Alberta plates would stick out around here, left behind in the parking lot by the cafeteria building, known as "the kitchen" in track speak.

The gravel on the road's shoulder scuffed the soles of boots that weren't made for walking, fingers wrapped around the harness of his helmet. Geai had told him to bring it. Did that mean he'd be getting on a horse?

There was no way of avoiding the glances that landed his way — curious, skeptical, amused. He returned the occasional *"Morning,"* some greetings clipped, others sing-song, and breathed it all in: the dust, the pungent aroma of the soiled bedding heaped in bins in front of each barn, the mingling of diesel — and jet fuel, from the airplanes that occasionally roared overhead as they landed at the nearby Pearson Airport.

All the barns he saw were the same — white cinderblock with pale green steel roofs, stall doors and trim painted a forest green.The buildings were kind of H-shaped with a short bit jutting from what would be the letter's bar — tack rooms and offices, not stalls. There were large shipping containers in the crowded bays, a groom carrying a bale of straw from one of them tipping him off they were for hay and bedding storage. Those bays were alive with horses being bathed, horses being hosed, horses being grazed; banter volleying between grooms and hotwalkers as they cared for the stars of this production. There were over a thousand horses back here, he'd read.

The large number five painted on the end of his destination was impossible to miss, but the sign hanging outside and the plaques on the stall doors weren't for Triple Stripe. They must be at the other end. Cutting through the barn would have made him feel too conspicuous, so he went the long way around.

These shedrows were prime: their view was the quaint tree-lined path that led to the main track, the grassy bank of the E.P. Taylor turf course rising behind it and blocking the view of the track itself. They had actual lawns instead of the strips of grass in front of those shedrows in the bays. Decorative bits of white fencing. Flowers hanging just beneath the overhang — though he'd noticed those at other barns as well. Even in the middle of a busy morning, everything was relatively neat. He could feel the pride.

It was a relief when he saw Emilie. He hadn't been sure

she'd be here, though she said she often came in on weekends. He needed his ally, feeling at the moment like a fish who'd been plunked in an unfamiliar pond.

"Nate!" she called, waving with one hand while the other held a loop of leather shank attached to a horse dark with bathwater. "Get over here so we can put you to work."

He would be all for that, because standing around looking awkward and out of place was not a fun prospect. *Put me on the end of a shank; better yet, put me on a horse so I don't look like a presumptive fool for having brought my helmet.*

The groom sloshing suds over the horse straightened as he approached, while the horse merely cocked an ear back and rolled an eye.

"This is Jo, Roger's assistant." Emilie kept one eye on the horse as she made introductions. "This is Nate, Jo. He's the one doing the yearlings this year."

Jo held out a hand, which was wet and rough when he grasped it. She was about his height, her mousy brown hair short, and she looked as if she didn't care that she was attractive and probably never stood still for long enough for anyone to make a proper assessment. Her life was likely perpetual motion.

"Hey," he said.

"Nice to meet you." She gave him a brief but not unfriendly smile before reaching for the sponge again.

"What can I do?" he asked, preempting any other line of questioning, thankful Jo was absorbed enough in her duties on a hectic morning not to engage in small talk or investigation.

"We've only got a couple more sets to go. It goes faster when Em and Liv are here to help. But I'm sure we can find one for you to get on. Are you licensed?"

He shook his head in response. "Not yet."

Jo barely hesitated, now running the sponge down the

horse's long tail, leaving a trail of bubbles. "If I put you on a horse you have to promise not to get hurt, then."

That got her a crooked grin. "I'll do my best."

"Put him on Paz," a figure surfacing from the shedrow said.

Nate heard a snort from behind the tall, dark-haired man who'd spoken — he looked too young and his clothes too worn to be the trainer, but who knew — then Liv appeared behind him. Her grin made Nate pause. Clearly she was more comfortable in this company than she'd ever been in his.

"That works," she said, the smile still flirting with her lips. Liv's more relaxed twin, maybe?

"Who's Roger supposed to get on, then?" Jo was rinsing now, her movements efficient. She was one of those people who managed not to get bathwater all over herself in the process of the post-gallop ritual.

"The stable pony?" Nate's eyebrow quirked. *Really?* That was a slap in the face. Pony was what racetrackers called anything that wasn't a racehorse.

"Part-time pony," Liv clarified. "He's not officially retired yet. He's also the one in the barn most likely to run off with you."

"So, this is like a test? An initiation?"

"Make sure you get him an orange vest," the tall guy said, cackling as he walked away. Nate wasn't sure he liked him, whoever he was.

Next, someone was going to ask him to go find the key to the quarter pole, he was sure. Some left-handed stirrup leathers, maybe? Or was it reins? And a saddle-stretcher. Did anyone play those pranks on backstretch newbies anymore? Yeah, he wasn't that green.

Another figure emerged from the shedrow and joined the little group — a tall man with neat greying hair, late forties maybe, wearing jeans and a polo shirt. *Roger,* Emilie mouthed to Nate. The trainer; head dude.

Roger looked from Liv to Jo. "What are we doing?"

Nate was trying not to laugh now. It was all beginning to feel like a comedy act. He almost glanced around for a hidden camera. Was he on an episode of *Just For Laughs* here?

"We'll work Just Stellar right after the break, then Paz can go with Toby. Put the tack on him, Michel?" Jo called after Tall Guy. A groom, then.

Emilie handed the horse off to a hotwalker, and assumed her Welcome Wagon role, formally introducing Nate to Roger. She pronounced his name the way Liv and Geai had — the French way.

"Usually we just call him Rog." The way she said the short form sounded more English.

He exchanged a handshake with the trainer, but before either of them struck up a conversation, a phone rang and Roger produced one from a pocket, saying, "Excuse me," as he pressed it to his ear and wandered off.

When it was nearing eight-thirty, Jo legged Liv up onto a dark bay filly and started leading her to the track. Emilie grabbed his arm.

"Let's go watch. Just Stellar is a half-sister to Just Lucky, from Starway's first crop. She's almost ready to run."

Instead of following Jo and Liv with the horse, she led the way across the road and up some stairs to a set of bleachers — and a panoramic view of the entire race course. He stared across the expanse. Three different racing surfaces, the land-scaped infield with its ponds and gardens and row of flags. A scene he'd only seen on television, and from the point of view of the towering grandstand. It took his breath away for a moment; dredged up the essence of the dream of it all. Riding here, at this place. The biggest track in Canada, and one of the top ones in all of North America.

Emilie brought him back to the reason they were out here, pointing off to the left. It took him a couple of seconds to identify Liv on the filly, jogging in the opposite direction, staying to the outside rail. Traffic on the main track was light right after the scheduled break for conditioning, but the numbers were steadily increasing.

"They're going five furlongs," Emilie said, which meant they'd be starting the breeze almost in front of where he and Emilie sat, five-eighths of a mile from the finish post on the other side of the track.

It was a few minutes before he found Liv again, coming around the turn towards them, now at a gallop. She stood up there like it was her favourite place to be, like whatever created that barrier when they were on the ground got left behind at the tunnel to the track. Like she belonged there. Like he felt. He shook off a strange kindred spirit feeling.

As the filly neared the black and white pole the clocker would start timing from, Liv dropped Just Stellar to the inside rail, her own body compressing as the filly's stride expanded. He thought he looked pretty good on a horse, but she made him feel like a complete imposter. And like maybe vet school was not where she was meant to be. But he kept that thought to himself.

Neither he nor Emilie moved until they'd watched Liv pull Just Stellar up, turning in to face the infield near the outside rail. When Liv guided the filly through the off-gap, Nate and Emilie climbed down from the bleachers and were back at the barn before horse and rider arrived.

"Nice filly," Nate said.

Jo led them again, Roger walking next to her, Liv looking tall and untouchable up there, her face still flushed from the work. Jo stopped Just Stellar on the apron in front of the barn where buckets of bath water waited. Liv hopped off and began removing the tack, a hotwalker appearing to hold the filly.

"Pony's ready," Michel called from where he stood inside the barn. Nate didn't miss the smirk Michel tossed his way.

"So, if security catches Nate out there without a license, who pays the fine?" Emilie quipped.

Jo scowled. "Just try not to attract attention."

"No one's trying to get you injured, Miller," Liv assured him.

Nate wasn't so sure. Plus, Miller? We were on those terms now, were we? It implied a familiarity he hadn't thought they'd achieved yet. It made him feel a tiny bit accepted, though. Like he was being incorporated into this tight-knit group.

"Good to know," he responded. Guess it was time. He pushed his helmet on and followed her onto the shed.

He studied the gelding as Michel brought the horse around. Paz was like the photo you might see under "Thoroughbred" if you googled it. Sixteen-one, dark bay with a fist-sized splotch of white in the middle of his forehead, one sock behind. He had a classic head and average build, and he was a little tucked up, so maybe he was fit. Michel stopped him in front of the tack room where Nate waited, and gathered the shank in his left hand, ready with his right to give a leg up.

"A ring bit?" Nate questioned. The bit the so-called pony wore was what they often used on a tough horse. This was no friendly rubber D.

"You'll thank me later."

Great.

Michel narrowed his eyes as Nate lifted the flap of the exercise saddle and checked the girth. Ran the stirrup iron down and checked the leather before adjusting the length. Reached up and checked the fit of the bridle. Walked around in front and checked the iron and leather on the other side before pulling it down.

"You don't think I can put tack on?" Michel snapped.

"I'd be doing the same if I put it on myself. Don't take it personally, buddy. Good job with the pads, though." Michel had tucked them nicely up into the gullet of the saddle. He collected the lines in his left hand, reaching his right for the back of the saddle and cocked his leg. Michel glowered and tossed him up. Good thing Nate had bounce, because Michel wasn't — purposely, Nate was sure — putting much effort into it. The groom turned the horse loose after a couple of steps, before Nate had even knotted the long, thick, rubber-gripped lines.

"Don't die out there," Michel said over his shoulder.

"Thanks for the vote of confidence."

Nate snugged up the girth after tucking his feet in the irons, then hesitated. Should he ride short? Long? He decided to ask Liv, who had called "Right behind you," shortly after Michel had legged him up.

"Paz doesn't care," she said.

He tried to study her face, but gave up figuring her expression out. Once they were on the horse path on the way to the track, he attempted another question.

"So if this pony runs off with me for a quarter he's not going to self-destruct?"

"No," Liv said. "He can handle that. He might run next weekend. It could be just what he needs to pick his head up."

Was she serious? Or joking? He couldn't tell.

He noticed few people talked to her but caught the looks landing on the two of them. Would the regulars know this was the pony he was on, even with the disguise of racehorse tack? Let's just get branded the new kid right off the bat. *Blessed are the meek, Miller.* You're doing this for a reason. One day, after he made it, this was going to be his Woodbine Racetrack origin story. *Yeah, they put me on the pony and told me not to get run off with.*

He was relying on her to know where to go, though it was easy to figure it out. He kept one eye on her, jogging when she jogged, staying on the outside rail, going the wrong way — clockwise — past a huge building on the left. She didn't start a conversation, so he kept silent, which left him to focus on Paz.

The gelding tucked his head, the weight of it in Nate's hands. He kept his knuckles pressed to the gelding's withers and breathed, and Paz snorted back. He liked to sing when he jogged; felt it relaxed the horses. But he wasn't quite ready to be that guy. Plenty of time to embarrass himself later. At least he hoped there was.

He was still staring up at the grandstand, taking in the multiple tiers, when she slowed her horse and turned forty-five degrees from the rail, so he followed suit. They were almost at the wire, and he stared some more at the landmark pole he'd watched horses flash past on Queen's Plate broadcasts and the Woodbine livestream, which he'd watched during those stretches where he was feeling inspired enough to think he might come here one day. Here he was, gazing at the big tote board behind it on the other side of an inner track. A jet roared overhead, descending into the airport. The horses didn't bat an eye, but Nate gazed up at it.

"Let's go," Liv said. "A mile and a half."

He nodded, his head snapping back to her. She was all business; no amusement at his gawking like a country boy in the big city. He wasn't a country boy — he'd lived in the suburbs of Calgary — but spending most of his free time on Al's farm, then all of it in the past eight months, he guessed the label was appropriate.

He was on the inside now. Paz seemed happy enough to

stick with his company around the clubhouse turn and into the backstretch. Nate tried not to notice that Roger had come out, standing on the rail chatting with a couple of other trainers as his eyes stayed locked on the new kid galloping his pony. Nate set his jaw again and forced his own eyes forward.

Paz rocked beneath him in more of a hobby-horse canter than a decent gallop. He wasn't taking a hold at all. They'd been having him on. He probably could have gotten this one around riding off the neck strap. When Liv's horse went faster, Paz lagged.

"Come on, old man," he hissed, hoping the wind caught his words so Liv didn't hear him. She did glance back, though. She didn't look concerned, and Paz picked up the pace, feeling a bit more like a racehorse. The horses breaking off to breeze at the five-eighths pole probably helped. Paz swapped leads heading into the turn and gained momentum as another worker zipped past on the rail. Now the gelding was taking a hold. He was into this. He was going to make Nate's arms burn. Arms that hadn't had much demanded of them by the yearlings. The bales of hay he'd tossed around helping with the second cut had done way more.

"Heads up," Liv called over.

They were midway around the turn and the sight of the grandstand looming again captured him. It was empty, of course. Even Paz's ears flicked forward, his head coming up a couple of inches. He drifted toward the inside rail slightly. Nate corrected him — then realized what Liv's warning had been about.

Three horses, breezing abreast, were sprinting from the quarter-mile chute — the very place they positioned the starting gate for the Queen's Plate. He'd been too spellbound by his surroundings to notice the schooling going on. Paz locked on at the quarter pole — that big, wide lane of a homestretch opening up before them, calling his name. The old horse drove into the bit and took up the chase.

And, now it's happening. I'm getting run off with by the pony. So much for not attracting attention.

Liv had warned him. And said the horse could handle it. He might as well make it look as if it was on purpose, and look good doing it. "You wanna breeze? Let's do this, old man."

So he crouched, his body still as he hovered over the saddle and let the wind rush by his ears. Paz pinned his back, his neck stretching with each stride as he ate up the track. Nate realized Liv was next to him, her horse travelling easily. They weren't going that fast, not much more than a two-minute lick, really. Liv picked it up a notch and Paz matched strides with his company.

When they pulled up on the backside, Liv was grinning at him. Well, if that's all he had to do to get a smile out of her...

"He's all right," Nate said. "Can he run a bit?"

"He can. He's just feeling his age. We haven't quite convinced him it's time to retire, though."

"So, do I get the call?" he quipped, and she actually laughed.

"They caught a time on that," Roger said as he fell into step next to them on the walk back. "I think I just might enter him Friday."

"Hey — I thought this was about me?" Nate said. Might as well run with it. "How did I look?"

Was that an eye roll he caught in his peripheral vision? In another five years, maybe she'd warm up to him.

"I've already got my help lined up for this winter," Roger said, "but if you're still with us in the spring, come gallop for me."

"Thank you."

"If we're ever short-handed one morning, maybe we can get you out of doing stalls and you can help us here for a few sets."

He didn't mind doing stalls, but he wouldn't say no. Michel met him with a halter when he followed Liv onto the apron in front of Barn Five. His feet were already out of the irons and he hopped off.

"You're welcome," Michel said as Nate slid off the bridle with that ring bit.

"Not that it did me a lot of good." But he grinned.

The looks that came his way as he walked back to the car were still there; maybe more curious now that the helmet was actually on his head. He slid it off and ran a hand through his damp hair, tossing the helmet onto the passenger seat of the Mustang. He'd grab a coffee before heading back to the farm to do the yearlings.

Pushing through the doors, he felt heads lifting and turning, eyes on him again. Assessing, speculating. At the end of the morning, the track kitchen was moderately busy. Once the races started, he'd bet it was full. He joined the short line and filled a cup with coffee once it was his turn.

"Be careful of that stuff. It's kinda toxic."

He jumped at the voice, not having noticed the man behind him — incidentally, with his own cup of the brew he'd just warned Nate about.

"Thanks for the heads up," Nate said, passing a five to the man at the cash register and dropping a loonie from the change into the tip cup. Extra sugar then. "The cream safe?"

"What's your name, kid?" The man was still next to him, doctoring his own cup. "You looked good out there."

Nate raised an eyebrow, stirring in the additions. He took a cautious sip and shrugged before responding carefully. "Thanks?"

"My name's Trevor Cobb."

He grabbed the man's offered hand and shook it. "Nate Miller."

"Never seen you around here before. Where you from?"

"Calgary."

"You ride out there?"

"Nope. Just gallop."

"How'd you get in with Triple Stripe? They don't have much turnover in that outfit."

"I'm starting their yearlings." Probably best to see where this was going before he confessed he was also just general barn help. "What do you do?"

"I'm an agent. Let me buy you a real coffee sometime, okay? Here's my number."

Well, this guy is forward. Trevor waited until he pulled out his phone and brought up his contacts. Nate punched in the number as Trevor recited it, then he sent the guy a text so Trevor would have his number too, because it seemed like the right thing to do. Building connections, right?

Trevor slapped him lightly on the arm. "See you around, kid."

CHAPTER EIGHTEEN

"DRAW THESE UP?" the technician asked. "It'll go faster if you help. Then you'll go with Parker, and I'll go with Dyna."

Liv usually helped Jake after galloping in the mornings on the weekends, but Jake was away for a wedding, so he'd told Liv she'd be working with another vet in the practice today. Dr Parker Baines was one of the most popular veterinarians at Woodbine, working for several of the top outfits. And that's what it was, she'd long ago realized. The vets worked for the trainers, at least in barns like those.

She was around enough to have heard the buzz on the backstretch. Not from Jake — he would never talk about a colleague like that. Baines was known for being current on all the latest treatments coming up from the US — the things the drug testing hadn't caught up with yet. It was no secret many trainers used him because they'd heard he gave horses an edge.

For that reason, today promised to be educational, even if it was in a way she didn't like. But it was important to be aware of such things. It was all fine to want to be on the side of the clean people in racing, but it did no good to ignore that not everyone was that way. Lines were danced upon, vets and trainers some-times doing precarious trapeze acts. Things that weren't neces-sarily illegal, but were they ethical?

She had to clear her mind of it; needed to remain impartial as she assisted him, so she let her mind drift back to simpler things as she inserted a needle through the rubber seal before tipping each corresponding bottle of medication to fill the syringes. Just Stellar had worked great. And Nate Miller had looked pretty good out there — even if he'd just been on the pony — though others had noticed. It felt wrong to want to keep him on the farm. Selfish. Not that she really had any power to do that. She was certain Roger would enter Paz for a race the same day as Just Stellar. He was sound and clearly still enjoying himself. The day he didn't try to run off was the day he'd be retired.

Dr. Baines swept into the trailer with a bustle of self-impor-tance. He was one of the younger vets around; in shape, his hair still dark, though there was grey in his meticulously trimmed beard. He wore a navy polo shirt — an actual Ralph Lauren one, with the tiny polo player logo — tucked into leather-belted beige khakis. She didn't know watches well enough to recog-nize the brand of the big timepiece on his wrist, but she was sure it was expensive. Part of his uniform of success. She couldn't imagine him ever getting dirty.

He was perfectly professional as they travelled in his black SUV to begin the late-morning rounds. The first few stops were routine pre-race stuff. Every medication name she didn't recog-nize, she asked about, keeping her expression that of a dutiful student and filing the information away.

The next barn gave her a creepy feeling. The sandy shedrow was neatly raked, everything put away, horses snoozing or munching hay, but it was deserted — not a groom in sight. Jack Faron specialized in claiming horses others had given up on and turning them around, some of his grabs tremendous success stories. He had the maximum number of stalls at Woodbine, another full string at the B track, Fort Erie, and who knew how many horses at one of the training centres where he had a whole barn to himself. Horses shipped in and out to breeze and race like they were on an assembly line. It was really no surprise Baines was his vet.

The technician at the trailer had warned her Baines worked quickly. With no grooms around, it was her job to hold these strange horses while he ducked in to jab them. Several of the animals anticipated Baines' abrupt bedside manner, spinning away or heading to the back of the stall as she entered. She tried to be both efficient and careful, so she didn't get herself kicked. She could feel the vet's impatience as she fumbled with the buckle halters — would it have killed the grooms to leave them on? Or was this on purpose, so the grooms were kept in the dark? All of it seemed very shady.

Baines paused once they finished the treatments and fired off a text. "We have one to inject. Katie will come hold him for us."

The technician appeared as Liv was gathering the chlorhexidine sponges to scrub the injections sites.

"You'll need lots," Katie said. "More than that."

The gelding Katie pulled from the stall was a plain bay, not a hair of white on him. Liv knew this horse. She and Geai had started him, back when Liv had time for that. Dean Taylor had bred him and sold part of him to one of his owners, like he did with many of their homebreds. He needed to, in order to survive most years. Sangria Factor had done well for them, finishing third in the Plate two years ago and after that regularly running in the money in stakes company. He'd even won a smaller stake race at Fort Erie last summer. But this year his form had fallen off. Trying to find an easier spot for him, Dean had run him in a claiming race. And Sangria Factor had been claimed, landing here. It felt as if she was running into an old friend in a place neither of them were proud of.

"What are you injecting?" she asked.

"Everything," Baines replied.

She tried to control the muscles in her face. Her job was to scrub, so scrub she did, Katie setting the timer on her phone to be sure she did it long enough. Parker was all tetchy energy, but she wouldn't be the one to skimp on this. It made her wonder how he was with his regular help instead of an impressionable vet student.

As she watched him inject every possible joint after she scrubbed each one, her stomach churned. *Get over it.* Her reaction was naïve. It probably happened every day, especially in a barn like this. Training couldn't accomplish that kind of short-term turnaround. Only drugs. Completely legal, as long as it was done far enough out from a race. Acceptable, though? While there was therapeutic justification for intra-articular injections, in her mind, this crossed an increasingly blurry line.

Would it bother her so much if she didn't know the horse? She felt like a traitor, standing by, witnessing this. Is this what she wanted to be doing? Why was she going to vet school? So she could spend her life sticking the animals she loved with needles... for sport?

When she finally climbed into her own vehicle, she swallowed the last bit of tepid water in her bottle and pushed into the seat, pressing the back of her skull into the headrest. Her body was always tired these days, but today her mind was more taxed than usual.

She started the car, poking the automatic window button as she blasted the air, even though it would take a few minutes to cool down. She wanted to get away from this place, back to the farm. Ride Claire. Hang out with Geai. Decompress. Maybe after that she'd be able to process this; clear her head enough to figure it out.

A tap on the driver's side window made her jolt to alertness, but she blew out a breath of relief, seeing it was Dean. Anxious feelings returned, though, when she remembered Sangria Factor. She wanted to tell him. She couldn't. And what would it change, anyway? Dean didn't have the money to claim the horse back, especially because the whole idea of doing all those injections was certainly to start the horse soon, which meant Faron had to run the horse up a level from the one at which he'd been claimed. Those were the rules. He would have to wait thirty days until the horse was "out of jail," as they said, to run back in the same class.

She pressed the window button, and it hummed back down. "Hey, Dean."

"A little jumpy?"

How did she answer that? Deflect. "And I don't even drink caffeine." She gave him a smile. It was a tired smile, but he'd understand that. He'd been up since four, too.

Would it be completely crazy to ask her father to claim the horse? There was no story that would explain it, though. And somehow that would probably get her in trouble. It would look fishy. Her father didn't claim horses. And there was no room for sentiment in her job. In this business. In her future.

Dean leaned down, resting his fingers on the edge of the car door. "I talked to the guy that owns..." He hesitated, like he was searching for a name. "Albert. That's what your guy calls him, right?"

Her guy? But she knew what Dean meant. Figure of speech. "Arthur," she corrected and waited for him to continue.

"He said it's his fault the colt is so backward, so however long it takes. I need more owners like that."

She smiled in sympathy. "That's great. I'll pass it along."

He straightened, but paused. "You okay?"

"Just ready to get home."

"All right. Have a good day."

At home, she showered to rinse off the morning's dust and sweat before opting for a swim. Her brain probably wouldn't even work enough to talk to Geai without a run or some lengths to settle it. The September humidity persisted, but it wouldn't last forever. One day she'd talk her father into heating the pool, but for now she had to take advantage of the weather.

Geai was in his chair watching the Woodbine livestream with Napoleon devotedly at his feet when she arrived. She'd done this so many times, sitting on his couch, analyzing and talking race strategy. This would be her homework if she were to become a jockey, not working for slick vets. Geai was the only one she could tell about this morning. He'd understand. He listened silently while she told him about Sangria Factor.

"What am I doing, Geai? All this work, all these courses. Courses on ethics! Are there enough people who don't want to train like that for me to even justify being a track vet?"

His response was frustratingly unsympathetic. "You think if you ride racehorses you're not going to find yourself in positions you don't want to be in? You think in any part of this business you're not going to have to stand up for what you think is right?"

Of course that was true. She sighed. "Part of me doesn't want to be in horses at all."

He just laughed at that. Napoleon thumped his tail in agreement. "I think all this angst about becoming a vet is just an excuse."

She frowned, her brow furrowing. "What?"

"An exit strategy."

"Don't talk riddles with me."

"You're not in vet school for you."

They'd never directly discussed it. Only Geai knew her well enough to guess the truth. The ridiculous truth.

"They gave up so much for me, Geai. Don't I owe it to them?"

"Owe it to them to be miserable? They gave it up because they had to. To remove you from something toxic."

"Isn't that reason enough to give up what I want?"

It was true, she admitted then. She was looking for someone to release her from her fate, but it wouldn't be Geai. He left her to figure that out for herself.

CHAPTER NINETEEN

"Dress nicely," Emilie had said.

"Please don't tell me that means a suit." Because the only one he owned was still jammed into the bag he'd shoved it in since he'd shed it after the wedding. Getting it to a dry cleaner hadn't been a priority.

"That's what my father and Roger will be wearing. If you want to go up to the Turf Club, you have to wear a tie, at least."

"Is it okay if I don't want to? I don't really think it's appropriate."

"I just didn't want you to think you're not welcome. Suit yourself."

"Or not?" He grinned.

He'd opted out of the suit and Turf Club and turned down her offer for a ride. If he drove himself, he wouldn't be obligated to stick around afterward and could do some exploring before. Get there early and not be restricted to keeping their company. He appreciated the invitation but wanted the freedom to spend the time there his way.

Triple Stripe had two runners at Woodbine today: one, Just

Stellar, a promising two-year-old at the beginning of her career; the other, Pas Encore, a war horse reaching the end of his competitiveness. While the filly commanded the services of Woodbine's top rider, the old gelding got the newest, lightest jockey in the room. Nate met up with Emilie as they brought the horses over for the filly's race.

"You have to come in the paddock," she insisted.

"I have to?"

"You're a big party pooper, you know?"

He laughed. "All right. Just because you asked."

No one knew him except the Lachance family and the Triple Stripe crew, but that was something. At least he wasn't a total outsider, but he still felt self-conscious as she ushered him into the huge walking ring, its trademark weeping willows sweeping overhead.

Just Stellar's race was the seventh on the card, a maiden allowance for two-year-old fillies going long — a mile and a sixteenth. She was second choice, trainer Roger Cloutier known for doing well with first-time starters. The favourite, Merry Merry, had a bridesmaid record: four straight second-place finishes.

Nate shook Claude Lachance's hand, then Roger's when the trainer appeared at the same time as the filly. Just Stellar looked just that — stellar. He could watch that filly all day. She was lovely, tall and dark and leggy in a Ruffian kind of way. She was going to be tough.

Liv appeared distracted as they waited for the riders, acknowledging his arrival with a mere nod. She kept her eyes on Just Stellar as the filly circled around them, led by the assistant trainer he'd met last weekend, Jo St-Laurent.

"Where's Geai?" Nate whispered to Em, like he felt he needed to be quiet.

"He never comes to the races. He'll watch at home."

He remained slightly behind Emilie, detached from the ones who belonged. He should be on the other side of the hedge, watching from the outside, looking in. This felt like a fishbowl, like he was being watched too.

Dave Johnson was one of the last jockeys to come from the room, striding over to the Triple Stripe group. He tucked his stick under his arm as he first greeted Claude, then nodded at Liv and Emilie before turning to Roger and shaking the trainer's hand. The rider's eyes barely brushed over Nate.

He wished he could jump in and do something with the horse. He didn't have a part to play and was conscious of not wanting to get in the way. Finally, the huddle broke up when the paddock judge called for riders up, Roger and Johnson stepping forward to the moving filly, the trainer legging Johnson up on the walk. Just Stellar settled into a bouncy prance, nose tucked, neck bowed.

"C'mon," Emilie said, nudging him as the horses filed out of the walking ring on their way to the track. Liv seemed to disappear, and Emilie noticed he noticed. "Too much nervous energy to stay stuck behind the slow people. She'll meet us at the seats."

"Permission to be excused from the post parade?" Nate said, lips twisting.

Emilie laughed. "Kind of."

The seats were in one of the outdoor boxes instead of the general seating on the second floor. Nate hesitated as the others filed in, but Emilie propelled him forward.

"You're bossy, you know that?" he said.

"Only because you need so much direction. Seriously."

Liv already perched on the edge of her post, a small set of binoculars pressed to her eyes and trained on the horses, now escorted by track ponies, jogging up for the post parade.

Once the race started, he lost his feeling of being out of

place. Up here, even though it was a box, they were all the same. A group of people who loved this game, on their feet screaming their shared favourite home. Emilie clutched his arm as she jumped up and down, shooting a fist into the air when Just Stellar hurtled to the finish in front.

Everything settled back to how it really was as he followed the troupe down to the winner's circle. Claude and Roger led the way, Liv hovering behind — with them but not — Emilie dragging Nate because of course he had to be in the win photo too. So he stood on the fringes and wondered if the photographer caught him smiling or looking lost.

Paz was in the last race, so there was an hour and a half to kill before then. It gave him a chance to wander and check things out, though he joined Roger and the Lachances again to watch the featured stake race and followed them downstairs afterward for the paddock ritual again.

Nate had already seen the entries and didn't recognize the name of Paz's rider, though he noted the low weight assignment with the number ten superscript next to it. An apprentice still riding with the full ten pound allowance a newbie received until he or she had won five races. Now that Nate had a program, he saw the kid's stats. Hadn't even *ridden* five races yet. That meant he didn't even get a whip.

"A triple bug?" he muttered.

"All the better for Paz to run off with." Liv slid her eyes his way, a crimp of her lips on one side.

He laughed, and tucked the program back under his arm, jamming his hands in his pockets, relegated once again to feeling mildly awkward.

That could be you.

The thought popped into his head, from where he wasn't sure. These people — Claude Lachance, Roger Cloutier — might very well hold his future in their hands. If he stuck with this operation, would they give him a leg up? Just because the two sisters seemed to regard the barn's regular journeyman with subtle disdain didn't mean there was room for someone new to wedge his way in. And this bug, whoever he was, was here already. Maybe he'd be Woodbine's next new star. He'd at least started on that road, while Nate stood here wondering about it.

He watched the rider approach, the kid looking so gaunt Nate thought the guy might pass out. When the apprentice joined the group, after first greeting Roger, who introduced him to Claude, the kid made the rounds. Liv was almost friendly with him. Emilie was a little flirty. It caught Nate off guard when the same hand was thrust toward him. No one introduced him or explained his presence, but it was always best to err on the side of caution when you were a brand new bug building relationships, he supposed. Nate took note, and suppressed a smile, thinking of Lucy, the butter tart lady. You never knew who might be your friend, so best to treat everyone you met with respect.

Paz was more on the muscle than Stella had been, bouncing next to the Triple Stripe swing groom with the assistant trainer Jo, on the other side. Nate got shuffled back in the press of bodies after the riders were up and Emilie caught his eye and called over her shoulder, "Meet us upstairs!"

He would have liked to have ignored that command. He wanted to watch the race by the rail with the common folk, because that's who he was. The second-floor box gave a better sightline, sure, but it wasn't where he belonged. Besides, the apron felt like a more appropriate place to watch the performance of an old workhorse like Paz.

"This horse have a shot?"

He snapped his head over his shoulder in time to see the

guy he'd met in the kitchen the other morning and snatched the name from his memory. *Trevor.*

"He's the pony," Nate chortled.

"Had a good move the other morning."

The guy said he'd seen Nate that morning. Did Trevor know this was the horse he'd been on?

"He likes to run off in the morning." Nate wasn't going to tell this guy he'd placed a few bucks on the old horse. Call it moral support, or a gut feeling. Either way, he had a soft spot for Paz.

Trevor fell into step beside him. "What are you doing breaking yearlings? I could get you on some horses if you want to ride. Take you to Fort Erie; do it on the QT so as not to ruffle the feathers of your farm people. Bet you could be riding races before the end of the season."

"I've got to meet them upstairs. Might get lost, you know."

"Don't forget to call me," Trevor shouted as bodies separated them.

Nate slipped into the back row of the box with Emilie and Liv, giving them an apologetic smile.

"You gotta keep up, Nate," Emilie said.

"Keeping up with you two is not an easy thing."

He and Emilie exchanged grins to Liv's wry eyebrow lift. If it wasn't for the physical resemblance, he'd wonder how those two were related. Liv fished her binoculars from her pocket and focused on the horses. Paz rocked next to his escort until the pony rider slowed him to turn for the post parade. Paz tucked his head into the pony rider's torso, getting a scratch on the forehead.

"He looks great," Nate said.

"That last breeze tightened him up nicely." Liv didn't remove the binoculars from her eyes, but there was that almost-grin.

The race was six furlongs, Paz's favourite distance according to his past performance. His odds dropped a little as post time approached, but he was still a longshot. It was a claiming race, but not the cheapest level at this track. The fact was, if they dropped him to a lower tag, he'd probably win, so there was more sentiment than solid business practice happening with this horse. At the right price, someone would snatch Paz up for sure, because there were a lot more steps on the way to the bottom, and the path there wasn't usually kind.

When the gates crashed open, Paz flew.

It was like with every stride, he increased his lead. Nate had eavesdropped in the walking ring, and the extent of the instructions Roger had given the kid were a shrug and a pat on the shoulder. All of them up here in this cramped box collectively held their breath, with glances at the tote board as it recorded Breeders' Cup Sprint-worthy fractions. Twenty-one and four for the first quarter. Forty-four and two for the half mile.

And Paz wasn't slowing down. At the head of the stretch, he was still soaring, his ears swiveling forward, probably catching the sound of his audience. He opened up still more.

The kid on his back looked as if he was afraid to move. Paz left the field far behind as he romped down the stretch, having his Best Day Ever. All of them were on their feet, Emilie bouncing as she screamed "Come on Paz!" Nate was speechless.

"Fifteen lengths. Eighteen!" The announcer called, his tone incredulous. "And at the wire, it's Pas Encore by nineteen lengths!"

Emilie threw her arms around Liv, then spun to grab Nate, both of them laughing. They spilled from the box, Emilie making him lead the way down the steps.

In the winners' circle, he kept a body-width from the others as they arranged themselves, the bug rider's teeth gleaming white against his dark skin, his eyes shining like today he was the star he surely expected he'd become. Emilie grabbed Nate's arm and dragged him closer before the photographer snapped the photos.

The money he'd just made on his bet had little to do with the fondness he felt for the old campaigner, and Liv's expression conveyed the same affection as she pressed past her father and Roger to reach Paz while the bug rider dismounted. Nate ventured up next to her to offer his own quick slap on Paz's damp neck, the network of vasculature popped, the horse's quick breaths pumping oxygen to his lungs.

"You sure he wants to be a pony?" he said, giving Liv a crooked smile as he ducked to the side, the swing groom sweeping Paz away — back to the stable area, to the test barn, where he'd be cooled out and post-race samples would be taken. There was probably a scad of people who'd watched that race wondering what the horse must've been on for the gelding to pull that kind of performance out of his tattered old hat.

Liv smiled. "We're playing that race-by-race. If he stays sound and keeps running off in the morning, he gets to run."

"Come back to the barn," Emilie said before he drifted too far away.

"Will there be beer?" Nate quipped.

Emilie snorted. "If there isn't, I can probably scare you up some, but I can't promise it'll be good. Should you be drinking when you're driving though, really?"

"I am so glad you're not really my girlfriend."

"In your dreams, Nate."

Back at the barn he nursed his beer — he felt he owed it to Paz to make sure first hand the old horse was okay after his afternoon caper. There was still grass on the lawn outside Barn Five, and Paz tore at it, his eyes bright with victory. There was no question in Nate's mind that horse was as proud of himself as his humans were of him.

A successful afternoon of racing for Triple Stripe. He was a visitor, allowed a glimpse, but he didn't belong. Tomorrow he'd go back to the farm job. Back to mucking stalls like the nobody he was. Back to the yearlings, doing the part of all this that no one would probably remember to give him credit for next year or the year after when those babies made it to the races themselves. He'd stand in front of a computer screen or television and think, "Hey, I started that horse," but his name wouldn't be anywhere in the picture.

When he said his goodbyes and climbed back into the Mustang, he sat behind the wheel, but before starting the car, he thumbed through the contacts on his phone, hovering over the number that agent, Trevor, had added. It must mean something that he'd run into the guy again today. A shove from above provoking him to get his ass in gear.

He pressed on the number and made the call. "I'm on my way out. Got time for that coffee?"

CHAPTER TWENTY

FAYE DOZED in the passenger seat while Liv drove, her friend's colossal travel mug resting in the console's cup holder next to Liv's water bottle. Liv liked the smell of coffee, but had never acquired a taste, even if there were times she thought caffeine might come in handy with her crazy schedule.

Her best friend was not a morning person. You would not see Faye at the track before dawn, so she and Faye had a deal — Liv drove to school and Faye drove home. That way, they each squeezed in more sleep, or more study, whichever was the priority. It was an hour and a half each way to the University of Guelph; not an insignificant journey. Sometimes Liv did both: sleep and study.

The weekend had gone by in a blink — and it wasn't the restorative time for her it might be for most students. So far this semester, she'd survived her determination to handle school, track and Claire, but she was only two weeks in and it was catching up with her. Saturday's all too practical education, working alongside Parker Baines, had taken a different kind of toll, but she'd had Sunday to work through it. Like Geai had said, she'd meet people she didn't like no matter what she ended up doing. Just because there were vets like Baines around didn't mean she would end up like him. Jake had asked her how it had gone, and she'd told him it had been fine and left it at that.

Faye stirred, straightening in the passenger seat. She reached for her mug and sipped. Even half-asleep, Faye looked more together than Liv ever felt. She turned up the stereo slightly, but not so much they had to talk over it.

"What do you have today?" Faye asked.

Liv recited the day's schedule, then reached for her water.

"The names of your courses make my head hurt," Faye said. "But, The Art of Veterinary Medicine? Do you get to draw pictures of animals or something?"

"I wish. You'd probably do better at that one than me. It's business, ethics and role playing." She cringed just thinking about it. Business and ethics, she was okay with. Role playing? Not so much. But it would probably be especially important to someone like her. She was beginning to understand life was often about learning to play the game, and this game, at least, had straightforward guidelines and lots of outlets for help. It was a system, and as long as you coloured within the lines, you were fine. You didn't have to like colouring.

"I don't know how you do it all," Faye said, stifling a yawn.

Where they left the car depended on who had the earliest class where. When it was Liv and they parked near Equine Guelph, the not-for-profit research centre, Faye would often go to the nearby Second Cup coffee shop and get some work done, or nap in the back corner, if she still needed sleep. Of course, Liv had more hours of classes than Faye did — it came with the territory. Faye didn't apologize for her easier schedule, but she did sympathize.

"Have a good day!" Faye called as she headed toward

College Avenue. It was rare they'd see each other until the end of it.

Play the game, Liv reminded herself as she found a place in class. This Art of Veterinary Medicine course was probably her toughest. She'd breezed through the math and sciences required during undergrad, and voraciously consumed anatomy and pathology, even relishing memorizing all the stuff she would never truly need to know for equine practice. She could communicate with written words, but the oral stuff — actually talking to strangers and saying what she meant — that was a challenge, like there was a barrier preventing words getting from her mind to her mouth.

Unlike Chad Winters, all smooth talk and easy body language. In a class year that was eighty percent female, he had most of the women smitten, though he was only sleeping with one as far as Liv knew. Liv also knew he couldn't understand why she didn't fall all over him like the others and seemed to resent her because of it. Not that she wasted much time worrying about it.

He was quick to call her on her connections — he'd made sure everyone knew about them — when he was just as, if not more so, connected himself. His father owned a well-known mixed practice in a rural community not far from Guelph. Add to that, there were so few men in the vet program anymore, sparkling prospects like Chad were cherished. The profs adored him as much as the female students did. He was their golden child.

He thought she was a snob. She thought he was a showoff. Their dislike for each other was mutual.

When the prof had discussed Emotional IQ during the first week of lectures, it had revealed her downfall, the glaring difference between her and Chad. She was probably smarter than him, but being smart wasn't enough. She could relate to animals all day long; would always have a kind word or a soft touch for them. Why did their humans have to be so difficult?

But, this course was supposed to help her with that, wasn't it? They could have written the first part of the curriculum for her. The fact the class existed indicated she wasn't the only one who struggled this way, wasn't it? She'd paid attention while Chad and his little harem of self-confident fans displayed expressions from boredom, to smugness, to thinly veiled mocking — while she sat on the other side of the room wondering if she could fail this course. That would solve the conflict about her future, wouldn't it?

They were starting the role-playing sessions this week — mock small animal appointments with actual actors. No doubt Chad would ace this. Maybe she wasn't planning to practice small animal medicine, but she certainly had to show she had some interpersonal skills for this exercise. She'd grown up in an animal-based environment that lauded hard knocks. Pet owners were a different species. Hearts trumped common sense way too often.

Though, Claire was exposing her own heart. Practicality be damned. Maybe she could conjure up those feelings to help her relate better.

Even as a child, she'd been aware: her grandfather was a businessman first. There had been no place for feelings. Everything she'd ridden had been for sale. Horses, horses, everywhere, and none of them were hers. Not that, other than creaky old Twizzle, any of them were hers now, either. Not even Claire.

She and Chad had that one thing in common, anyway: real-world exposure to the reality of this profession. No rose-coloured glasses on either of them, though by third year she expected the tint had worn away for most of the others as well.

Watching Chad Winters do his "simulated client interview" only made Liv's ineptitude even more obvious. She'd bet he'd taken drama; probably acted the lead in the school play every year of high school. She almost felt she should applaud when he finished. It reminded her coldly of Dr. Baines; a performance for the client. Not that she had any reason to suspect Chad would have a darker side behind the scenes.

It was her turn next, to be on the other side of this window while her classmates observed. Being seen when she couldn't see. Not the kind of lab she liked, but she put on the white coat like it cloaked her with confidence. Competence. Fearlessness. Just as if she were on the back of a horse.

But even before she met her assigned "client," she became much too warm, her pulse bumping upward at the thought of being in a confined space with a stranger. She wasn't exactly claustrophobic, but anticipating the sterile room and close walls triggered a mild flight response. The stranger wouldn't even have a pet, so there would be no buffer zone. Who had decided that? Something about this being a communication exercise and not wanting the distraction of an animal. She rolled her shoulders back and took a deep breath, pushing open the door, then, realizing her eyes had already dropped to the floor, forced them up and pasted on a smile.

It felt as if someone punched her in the solar plexus.

To anyone else, he probably looked like a benign older gentleman, but the resemblance to her less than kind grandfather made her stomach churn, the breath she sucked in forcing a small hiccup sound from her throat as her hand flew to her mouth. The room, the pressure, the flash of memory —all of it closed in on her. She stumbled backward against the door, mumbling, "Excuse me." Then, spinning, she rushed out.

The halls were empty, and she found a wall, braced her back against it, slid to the floor. Clutching her head in her hands, her heart pounded in her ears and she gulped for air. Was there no oxygen out here? It felt like someone had replaced it with carbon monoxide, her lungs deprived, her chest tight as a damp chill crept over her. *Breathe, you need to breathe... you aren't dying.* She forced herself to imagine she was running. Running required breathing. *Inhale, exhale...* but that just made her worse.

A horse. Imagine you're on a horse. Hacking Claire through the woods, the air warm, the shade dappled with patches of sunlight. Claire's respiration steady; consciously making hers match it.

Slowly, her heart rate settled. Control returned. She was aware of someone standing nearby. How long had they been there?

"Hey, Liv? Are you all right?"

Chad kept his distance, his face showing surprising compassion. He'd make a good vet, Liv decided. Knowing how to read animals enough to give them space when they needed it — even human animals — was important.

Was she all right? Maybe not entirely. Just better. But "Yeah," was the appropriate answer. She climbed to her feet, giving her spinning head a moment to regain its equilibrium. "Sorry, I feel a little ill. I must've eaten something."

Chad's expression suggested he wasn't convinced. "Can I call someone for you?"

"That's all right. I'll call my friend. We drove together."

"Okay. Good. I'll grab your bag for you and tell Dr Whittaker." He seemed glad to be relieved of any further responsibility, but she felt gratitude toward him just the same.

Faye was in the University Centre food court, coffee cup next to her phone, book bag resting at her feet. Liv mustered a smile. She had a lingering headache and felt worn out, and wished at that moment she liked coffee. Faye gave her an appraising look, then reached into her bag, extracting a half-eaten bar of dark chocolate.

"You look like you could use a pick-me-up."

"Thanks." The traces of caffeine and theobromine might be enough to get her through this. Faye was driving home though, so she could also just give in to the fatigue. Either way, chocolate was never a bad idea and the first taste of it melted slowly on her tongue, smooth and bitter.

They threw their bags on the backseat of Faye's Corolla and climbed in, Liv snapping the seatbelt in place and closing her eyes as the back of her skull pressed into the headrest.

"What happened?" Faye asked before she turned the key in the ignition.

How much to say? She drew in a breath. "The stress of everything is getting to me, that's all."

Faye quirked a perfect eyebrow, unconvinced, but commented, "You are trying to do a lot. But if you ever want to talk about it, you know... "

"I think..." She hesitated. "I think maybe I had an anxiety attack. We started those stupid simulated appointment things today. And I... I kind of flipped out. I bolted. I mean, I think I can fail that part and still pass the course, but I'm sure I'll have to make up for it somehow. They really, really don't want people dropping out, but this class is important."

"So, no easy escape?"

Liv opened an eye, catching the twist of Faye's lips, and decided not to answer. She didn't need any encouragement thinking about that, so best not to entertain it.

She closed her eyes and let Faye think she was sleeping. She felt hollow, but that hollow was the very place she'd put it all, once she packaged it up again, stuffed it back down, because this would not define her. There was no time or place for it.

Faye's voice roused her, and she realized she'd drifted off. She crawled out and tugged her bag from the back seat.

"See you in the morning, sweetie," Faye said. "Try to get some more sleep, okay?"

She gave Faye a tired grin. "If sleep could be optional, my life would be so much easier."

But right now, she wished she could sleep for days, not hours. And wake up on a beach somewhere where everything in her life made sense. She wished it were the weekend. She wanted some space between the embarrassment of this afternoon and when she had to face those people again. The episode had exposed weakness. She hated that.

If ever she'd felt like skipping her session with Claire, it was today. She was just so tired. But Claire was just what she needed right now. To resist any lingering temptation, she didn't even go into the house. Her boots and helmet lived in her car, so she gathered her keys from where they'd settled at the bottom of her bag and, in the name of saving energy, drove to the training barn. She quickly had Claire tacked up and headed out on a mind-clearing hack.

Claire picked her way carefully over roots and rocks along the trail through the woods. Liv tipped her head back and looked up through the leaves, the foliage so thick she only caught tiny glimpses of the blue, blue sky. The mingling scents of pine and wood and peat, horse and leather, were the incense for her meditation.

Her neck snapped forward as Claire stopped in her tracks. There stood Nate Miller, who had clearly done exactly as Claire had, near where the forest opened into the stallion barn and paddocks. He wore loose nylon gym shorts that nearly reached his knees, his t-shirt damp where it touched his chest.

If Claire could feel her thudding heartbeat, she wasn't showing any sign of it. The filly actually rocked forward, like she wanted to take a step, and only the lift of Liv's hand on the lines stopped her. Claire no longer thought of him as an intruder, only Liv.

"Hey," he said, running his fingers through hair darkened with sweat before using the sleeve of the t-shirt to wipe his face. He didn't approach, eyeballing her warily for a moment.

"Hi," she responded, thinking, *this is stupid.*

"Can I pet your horse?" Then Nate grinned.

The brilliance of his smile knocked her sideways, and she had no choice but to respond with one of her own, though its vividness would never compare to his at the best of times; eyes that were more cool grey than blue, no competition for his. Even from a distance, his looked a perfect colour match for the Caribbean.

"Sure. She'd like that. She likes people." Unlike her rider, but she kept that to herself.

He approached, his gait neither fast nor slow, and presented his palm to the filly. Liv gave with the reins as Claire dropped her head.

"Can I give her a peppermint?" he asked.

"You can try. She's never had one before."

She heard the crunch and caught a faint whiff of peppermint as Nate reached his other hand up to stroke Claire's neck. Go figure. It was like the filly had been eating them her whole life. He'd probably been sneaking them to her in the paddock all along.

"She's a sweetheart," he said, his eyes still on the filly, the fondness with which he looked at the yearling poking at a soft spot in Liv's heart.

"Do you always carry peppermints with you when you run?" she asked.

"I have a standing agreement with the broodmares. I can't let them down."

He stepped to the side and tossed a quick look up at her. The brilliance was gone — there was no display of that perfect set of teeth — but it was a wry look. The initial wariness had disappeared.

"Have a nice ride. See you around," he said, and carried on.

Glancing over her shoulder as she let Claire move forward again, she found he was doing the same — and she silently congratulated herself again on that hire. Not just because he was good with the yearlings and had a genuine affection for the horses. She liked him because he didn't ask questions. So many people over-shared. She didn't. He didn't. They'd get along just fine. If he stayed. He had the freedom to leave.

By the time she trudged up the front steps of the house, it was getting dark, a light illuminating the door. She slipped through, kicked off her shoes — boots and helmet stashed back in her car — and left her bag in the hallway before shuffling into the kitchen to refill her water bottle.

"I'm exhausted, Maman," she said, begging off sitting down to eat. "I'm going to just head up to bed."

Her mother came over and wrapped her arms around Liv's shoulders; a rare thing. "You're trying to do too much. I'll leave a plate in the fridge for you, in case you wake up ravenous later. If you don't eat it tonight, you can take it with you tomorrow."

"Thank you."

Liv let her head rest on Anne's shoulder a moment, feeling the rise and fall of her chest, and her mother's arms tightened briefly before letting go. Upstairs, after a shower and changing for bed, she tucked her legs under the covers, rested her laptop on her thighs and put Google to work. *Panic and anxiety. Symptoms and treatment.*

Counselling. Medication. Breathing exercises.

Claire was her anti-anxiety drug; swimming and running her breathing exercises. Today had been a wake-up call, that was all. She would move forward with the awareness it created. Be prepared. It was all mind games anyway, wasn't it?

CHAPTER TWENTY-ONE

HE'D ASKED for and been given Mondays off so he could get together with Will — Mondays traditionally a day restaurants closed. This week, though, after that coffee with Trevor, he switched his day off to Tuesday, set his alarm for stupid o'clock, and drove to Fort Erie. He was gone long before anyone on the farm had roused.

Will wasn't happy.

"Don't you see what you're doing?" he'd said when Nate had called him. "You're diving right into this. Do you know this guy? You have this perfectly solid job with what you keep telling me is a great employer, and you're going to toss that for this?"

"I haven't tossed anything yet. I've gotta keep my options open, right? You're just pissed I'm blowing you off."

"Sure, I'm pissed you're blowing me off. But it's bigger than that. It's your motivation. You're hurting yourself more than me."

"You're being dramatic."

"Whatever. Have a good time. Don't forget me when you're famous."

He refused to feel guilty about this. No one could tell him what to do on his day off. What had Geai said? *I don't believe in holding people back.* The old man obviously felt this farm position was below his pay grade. Seize the day, and all that. So what if a tiny voice in his head called it self-destructive? Or maybe that was just the echo of Will's words.

As he got closer to his destination, the green and white highway signs reminded him how near he was to the US-Canadian border. Lewiston. Niagara Falls. Then Buffalo. All three potential crossing points spelled opportunity. Better places to winter than a farm in Ontario. South Carolina, Arkansas, New Orleans... Florida. Little boxes on a list of possibilities.

The security shack at Fort Erie wasn't hard to find — it was just off the track's parking lot. He'd barely rolled down his window and opened his mouth, ready to proffer his license before the guard waved him in. Okay. Security was less of a thing around here.

The Fort Erie backstretch was culture shock after Woodbine; it didn't take him long to understand why one of the farm girls referred to it as "Fort Dreary." This place looked like a forgotten version of the fancier Toronto track, its glory days far in the past.

Famous. Yeah. He couldn't imagine finding a ticket south here, let alone fame. This wasn't his beautiful life. He didn't even want it showing up in his backstory, if he made it.

Unlike the landscaped aisles at Woodbine, the shedrows had deep grooves from the Thoroughbreds walking round and round, day in, day out. It made him ache for a load of sand and a hard rake. The green steel stall doors and white cinderblock walls needed fresh paint in the worst way. Weeds climbed the chain-link fence that enclosed the stable area. It reminded him a little of a prison. He shoved the depressing thoughts aside and found the kitchen, the Mustang creeping as he kept alert for horse traffic.

"Welcome to the Fort," Trevor said, sweeping his arms wide after they shook hands, like it was somewhere grand. "Ready to go?"

The barn Trevor took him to was a little better kept than some of the others. There were stall plaques on the doors and planters hanging between the posts of the outer rail, and the shedrow wasn't a complete disaster. The sign hanging at the end of the building read, "Jack Faron Stables," a Woodbine trainer who had enough horses to need stalls at both places. The Fort Erie division was the temporary home to horses at opposite ends of their careers: unraced two-year-olds and older horses who had dropped in class.

After introductions, the assistant called down the shed to a groom, "Bring him out, Crystal. Jock's here."

Nate's eyes shifted to Trevor, but the agent showed no admission of the truth he'd not even approximated. He'd play along if it meant he got to breeze a couple. It could be a foot in the door of a big stable for him.

"He was a good horse once," the assistant said. "He's got a couple more races in him."

Before he blows up into a million tiny pieces?

Nate frowned, watching the way the horse walked down the shed, hooves swinging and landing wide like his big old knees were bothering him. As the assistant threw him up, he tried to dismiss his concerns. Trevor and the assistant followed him to the track.

The racetrack made him rethink some of his earlier misgivings. Sure, the grandstand was a little run down, stuck somewhere in the seventies — or earlier, what did he know — but the infield was possibly more beautiful than Woodbine's, perhaps because it was quaint, with its little bridge. There were stories here. There was character. The stories at Woodbine had been renovated and replaced with slick concourses and a fancy casino.

The horse felt rocky when they started galloping — the assistant didn't even want him to jog to warm up. It scared Nate more than a little. What the hell was he doing here? He could be putting his life in danger, riding an unsound horse; it was like Russian Roulette. For what? A shortcut on a career path he was currently lukewarm about pursuing? But that's what he'd be doing every day of that career. Fear had no place. He said a quick prayer the horse had another half-mile work in him and dropped him to the rail at the five-eighths pole.

The old gelding felt better at speed, but the freaky-quickness was unsettling. Unsound horses ran from pain. The faster they went, the less it hurt, the adrenaline and endorphins taking over, banishing discomfort. A horse like this could break down underneath him and not feel a thing. *Tick, tick, BOOM.*

At least he didn't need to ask the gelding at all, because he was eating up the track, firing off the seconds at a pace that would meet the assistant's instructions. When they reached the wire, he rode the gelding through before standing in the irons, the horse's momentum carrying him around the clubhouse turn. Nate pulled him up as soon as he could and wished the gap wasn't so far away. They were sauntering at an easy walk when they rejoined the assistant and Trevor.

What this horse needed was a nice pasture with some buddies, and a teenage girl to dote on him and take him for trail rides. What he'd probably get was a round of joint injections, and at the end of the season, a one-way ticket somewhere Bute was legal so he could run on the anti-inflammatory drug until his body finally gave out. If he had the money, he'd claim the horse himself when he ran and secure the future the old gelding deserved. Maybe that was reason enough to pursue this now — to get to the bigger paycheque that would let him do things like that. He wanted to be that kind of rider — the kind that gave back. But maybe he was an idealistic fool and would end up jaded like the rest of them.

"That was great," the assistant said, rattling off the time.

The figure didn't surprise Nate. He shrugged. "I just let him do his thing."

He was pretty sure anyone could have, but he kept himself from saying what he'd joked after the Paz fiasco: *how did I look?* That was the point of him being here, wasn't it? Not getting a poor cripple through a half without flying apart.

"Got time for one more? My exercise girl bailed. Just needs to gallop."

Nate glanced at Trevor; not because he was looking for permission. He wasn't here to be someone's free gallop boy. But he was here to foster relationships.... even though he wasn't sure a relationship with this outfit was something he wanted to foster. He was starting to feel as if this was where Faron hid his dirty secrets.

He made as if he was checking the time, like he was in demand or something. "All right."

As he adjusted the tack before mounting, he couldn't help thinking, *how's this one going to try to kill me?* Turned out, that became apparent before they were even on the track: when they were still twenty feet from the gap, the colt went straight up.

Nate plastered himself against the horse's neck, his arms thrust forward so the lines were loose, and somehow got his feet under him, grateful at that moment he'd dropped his irons a couple of holes from the length at which he'd breezed the older horse.

There was a moment when time seemed to stand still as a

horse reared; a tipping point when you had to decide if you were going to bail or ride it out. *Should I stay, or should I go?* Pick one, and hope you made the right decision and didn't end up with the horse on top of you.

Maybe it was self-preservation, or maybe it was the thought of trying to explain to his actual employer that he'd injured himself while moonlighting, so they were going to have to find someone else to finish their yearlings. The cushy job, the nice apartment... he saw it all go *poof* in his mind's eye. So he stayed, not in small part thanks to the colt's incredible balance. He'd had practice, this horse. If he didn't want to be a racehorse — which at the moment seemed to be a hard, *no* — maybe he had a future in the movies.

When the colt came down after what seemed an impressive but breath-robbingly long time in the air, landing with himself still under Nate instead of the other way around — *win* — Nate was ready, horse and human hearts drumming in concert like timpanis. He couldn't give this colt time to think, or they'd be doing it all over again. So... forward not working? *Okay, son... we're going sideways.*

He threw an open rein to the left, using his right hand — the one with his whip — to shoo the colt. Away from that arm, away from the gap and the direction they were supposed to be going. As he drove with his left heel, kicking his feet free of the stirrups so he'd have more leg, he prayed he didn't regret that decision. The maneuver unbalanced the colt just enough to keep the ball in Nate's court. Then he pushed the colt around that inside leg, the two-year-old leaping into a jog. He didn't like working horses in tight circles, but in this case, he needed to keep his mount guessing.

He was going to be the crazy guy they were talking about after he left. The one schooling a two-year-old on a ten-metre circle in a cloud of dust. Once the colt was accepting to the left, he changed direction, and went to the right. With just enough awareness to stay out of the way of the horses who still headed for the track, their riders gawking, he picked up his irons and jogged the colt through the gap like they were coming down the centre line of a dressage test. As if he'd ever ridden one.

After that, heading onto the track seemed like a picnic. The oval wasn't busy anymore, so he backed the colt up into the chute, stopped to turn him with his butt to the outside rail and rubbed the hell out of his neck, admiring the trees and feeling the two-year-old's pulse settle with his own, both of them dripping sweat. Then he walked him to the gap and off the track.

The assistant was there, throwing his arms in the air. "Why didn't you gallop him?"

The colt shied and Nate channeled him forward. It was really, really tempting to hop off and throw the lines at this guy. *You get on him.*

"He had a nice time out there today." *Well... on the track, anyway.* "Maybe if you give him a nice time for a few weeks, he'll be happier about training. Obviously putting the rush on him isn't getting you anywhere, so what have you got to lose?"

He bit back the rest, though he guessed he'd already done enough damage to ensure he never rode anything in the Faron barn again. He wasn't sure he cared. He was supposed to be working horses, not installing basic software.

The assistant seemed to come around by the time they walked back to the barn, though, thanking him and asking if he'd be back tomorrow. *Uh, that's a no.*

Trevor followed him to his car. "I mean it, you could be riding by the end of the season. Then I'll set you up with a trainer going to Palm Meadows or Oaklawn to gallop for the winter. If Faron isn't looking, I know a couple others still needing help. You could be top apprentice next year."

Those were big promises, the names like places he'd only

heard of in fables; now his for the taking when he didn't think he'd done anything impressive except not die.

"I really want to go to California," he quipped to postpone a proper answer, tipping off his helmet and running his fingers through his hair, damp and plastered to his head. Underneath his safety vest, his t-shirt was saturated.

"You go there, you might never come back." Trevor grinned.

"True." He twisted the helmet's harness between his fingers, stalling. "I'll get back to you."

Was he crazy not to want that? Why not now? Trevor was offering the chance to be associated with a trainer with the highest win percentage at Woodbine. It was a big, shiny opportunity. It was a safe bet he wasn't going to like every conditioner he rode for. He'd have to pay his dues before he could pick and choose.

He needed to get out of here, find a convenience store and buy a big bottle of water; get himself hydrated so he could think properly. They didn't sell that size in the track kitchen, and he wasn't sure he'd want to make an appearance there anyway, after the attention he'd drawn to himself. It was starting to seem like every time he left the farm, he caused a scene somewhere.

As soon as he hit the highway, he realized just how much the morning had exhausted him, but he was too amped up to return to the farm yet. It was early still, and it was his day off, so he pulled off the highway at the exit for Niagara Falls.

It was packed with tourists. Here he could walk and not turn heads, though maybe he'd buy a souvenir t-shirt because the one he wore was gross after his unexpected workout. He took some photos with his phone, because that was what you did when you visited one of the world's wonders. And it was amazing despite the kitschiness of the town behind him — the thunderous rush of the falls, the rolling mist cooling him. In a moment of inspiration he started an Instagram post, then stopped himself, because though he had next to no followers, Emilie Lachance was now one of them. He didn't want to have to explain how he'd ended up here. He sent a photo to his mom instead. *Guess where I am? No prizes for the right answer.*

He made it back to the farm early afternoon. He should've gone for a run, but weariness caught up with him, the coffee he'd picked up for the drive home long since metabolized. The early morning, the excursion, the decisions that needed to be made.

Staring out the picture window as he towel-dried his hair after a shower, he felt the tranquility of this place. It soothed a soul that all too often seemed broken, but he'd get over that with time, not with pretty views. It wasn't necessarily right to be comfortable, because it would lead to complacency. Last time he'd found himself in that position — a year ago, it was just a year ago — life had beaten him down with a big stick.

If he waited until it was all just right to make his move, it could be too late. Around here it would be easy to think this was his future, then end up watching what could have been his life pass him by. And if he ended up crashing and burning — almost, if not quite, literally — that would show his ex she was wrong, and his father would take great pleasure in telling *him I told you so.*

His phone rang, the name on the caller ID relieving his overwrought brain, a smile coming immediately to his lips. "Hi, Mom."

"What were you doing in Niagara Falls?"

"Sightseeing. It was my day off."

"I know you take Mondays off, Nate."

Like he could keep anything from his mother. She'd never settle for the smartass answer.

"I was in Fort Erie, at the track there, getting on some horses," he admitted. "I met an agent — like a rider's agent — and he's trying to give me everything I thought I ever wanted." Before he'd decided he wanted a girl, one particular girl, more than anything.

His mother's hesitation was a giveaway. She knew it all, the whole sordid story, had watched it play out. "Is that what you still want?"

"Shouldn't I?"

"Nate." Called out on the smartass comment, again.

"Shouldn't I?" he repeated, but his tone did a one-eighty, painted this time with a plea; pain and desperation he couldn't submerge.

"Patience has never been one of your strongpoints. You could work on that. What's the hurry?"

The hurry was, he was twenty-three and most guys started riding at eighteen. The hurry was, if he stayed here too long, he could see himself becoming so comfortable he'd never leave, giving up on the dream altogether. Was this farm even reality, truly? The morning he'd spent at Fort Erie was a lot closer to the real world. Reality was calling. He needed to give it an answer.

CHAPTER TWENTY-TWO

THEY GAVE her a do-over for her appointment simulation. *Don't think, just do. Play the game, get the grade.* Same small room with the one-way glass, but a woman playing the part of the client. Coincidence? Probably not.

It was a relief when she took a seat with her classmates on the other side of the glass. Chad caught her eye and gave her a thumbs-up. She managed not to make a face, nodding and finding a small smile. Support came from the most unlikely places.

The actor joining the next student in the room was easy to recognize, but from this point of view, the older gentleman didn't set her senses into disarray. From here, the only resemblance he bore to her grandfather was his white hair and body shape. His expression, now that she actually watched his face, was softer, and his voice had a slight English accent. When she'd encountered him, she hadn't stuck around long enough to hear him speak.

Still, afterward, tension crept up her spine, into her neck, clustering at the base of her skull. She needed to test her coping mechanisms — needed to prove to herself she'd dealt with this.

She'd rehearsed an apology; written up a script and memorized it, doing a little play-acting on her own in case she faced him again. In real life, she wouldn't be able to prepare in advance for such things, so she hoped in time she'd get better at it.

She approached him and gave her speech without too much blundering. He was perfectly gracious, and she emerged on the other side still feeling uncomfortable, but it felt like a tiny victory just the same.

Claire was over a month into her training now, Liv starting the filly on a foundational conditioning program. Finally letting her gallop on the track — just a nice, easy canter — was the best ending to a stressful day. When she turned Claire back out with the other fillies, Claire dropped and rolled in the dusty patch near the gate, shaking it off in a cloud when she rose. It made Liv wonder what the human equivalent was to that clearly therapeutic action. Drop, grind away the day's stresses, then get up and shake it off.

A text notification from her father pulled her focus from the filly. "See you tomorrow, Claire," she called lightly, then turned and went to meet him.

When her father had business to discuss, more often than not, he asked her to meet him in the farm office. She appreciated he included her in these things, at least keeping her informed if rarely asking her to make final decisions. Hiring Nate had been the first time he'd left something up to her. He considered her ideas; had agreed with her admittedly sentimental argument to justify his own desire to breed Sotisse to Just Lucky. Sometimes you had to listen to your heart. They didn't have to cater to the whims of the commercial market, so they could take chances like breeding a maiden to a first-year stallion.

She was aware she was being groomed. Welcomed it. While her father wasn't terribly hands on, leaving most things to Geai and their trainer Roger, he was the guy with the money, so ultimately he ran the show. One day he'd step back and just be the bankroll behind the outfit, leaving Liv to assume said show-running... one day when she'd established herself as a veterinarian.

She silently acknowledged the oil painting behind the desk, her eyes remaining on it as she dropped into the overstuffed chair — the same one Nate Miller had occupied the day of the interview. He'd woven himself into the fabric of this place. Not that he was tied to it. Those threads were easily broken.

Her father was locked into something on the computer, so she let herself study the portrait. It had been important, of course, to find an artist who knew anatomy. Liv couldn't paint anything like that, but she'd judge the rendered figures as hard as she would real animals standing in front of her. She'd entrusted her mother, who had more of an artistic eye, to select potential painters, but she and Geai and her father had narrowed the shortlist to choose the one who depicted horses best.

Claude finally looked up, smiled at her, and sat back in his chair. She didn't know what this meeting was for. Perhaps to talk about breeding decisions for next year. School came under "family" so she endured those questions at meal times. It was the downside of living at home while she went to university; the trade-off for getting to spend time, any time, with Claire.

As usual, he didn't waste time getting to the point. They weren't dissimilar in that way.

"I've talked to Roger, and we're going to send Claire and

Gemma to Florida for the winter. Claire might be small, but you've done such a good job with her, and Gemma, of course..."

He didn't have to expand on the full sister to Just Lucky and she tuned out whatever he said next, the ringing in her ears distracting her. Claire was going to Florida. Without her.

"Have you decided on a name for her?" her father asked, the drone fading away.

Liv shook off her disappointment — an unwarranted emotion when she'd known better all along. Back to business. She often helped name the horses; everyone had assumed she'd christen Claire.

"L'Éclaircie," she said quietly. *The Lightening.* Because of the lightening the filly provided her heart, as ironic as that seemed at the moment.

Claude nodded. "Have you submitted it yet?"

She shook her head. "No. I will."

Her father left her there, in that room, her eyes returning to the painting of Just Lucky and Sotisse. Her father's legacy, that magical fusion of DNA growing inside the chestnut mare. If Claire wasn't going to fulfill Liv's dream, maybe that foal would. After all, she'd be done vet school by the time it was old enough to race. Surely she could manipulate her schedule once she was practicing to, at the very least, be the one starting it as a yearling.

Pushing herself up from the depths of the chair, she slipped around the desk to the seat her father had vacated and signed into the Jockey Club's interactive site, making a single name claim for *L'Eclaircie.* At the house, she changed into running gear, slipping in and out silently.

She ran to get away from the noise in her head. She ran for the endorphins, acceptable self-medication. She ran because it was solitary; there was no partner to steal your heart.

She felt things she had no right to feel. Hurt. Anger. This is what she got for letting herself get attached. Breaking bonds hurt when you were human, and she was feeling so disappointingly human right now. This was right for Claire. Sending the filly south wasn't part of her mother's plot to keep her focused on her degree, as easy as it would be to let herself think this was some kind of conspiracy. It was a testament to the filly's progress and potential.

If she didn't make it, Liv could claim her for her own; keep her to ride. Maybe she'd go back to eventing. She'd adopted Twizzle after her father had retired him from the track. He was her gateway drug to a faster, freer world than the hunters and jumpers she'd grown up with. It was a natural progression to racing, especially with Geai's ready encouragement.

Or, she could just be a casual rider. Not worry about ribbons and accomplishments, speed and adrenaline. In the end, it was about being together; sharing a heartbeat, right?

Would it be enough? Coming home after a long day and just riding? Not for the exhilaration, but for the companionship alone?

It was better this way. Once Claire was gone, she could immerse herself in her school work, because Claire kept that nagging voice in her head alive. The one that said *I'd rather be riding.*

She realized it, then. It wasn't so much about the filly herself, the heart horse status Liv had given her — it was what Claire embodied. She stood for everything Liv wanted, but could never have. Claire would go to Florida, then probably, next spring, to New York, if she continued to show promise. Liv had to let go.

Her head was down, negotiating that last big root jutting into the trail right before it opened into the weanlings' pastures, and she almost collided with him. His eyes probably hadn't adjusted to the shade, so he hadn't seen her either.

She didn't stop, and neither did he. He hopped to the side with a quick look, his expression mirroring hers — wary, humourless, no cheeky comments like *we have to stop meeting like this* — and she leapt forward, carrying on, his presence merely an impression, a flicker in her periphery, a trick of the light. Here one second, gone the next.

But it was as if an essence of him drifted in his wake and now wisped around her. Nate had dropped out of school to play with horses. He'd run away from the expectations. He was going after what he really wanted.

She'd heard more than rumours. He was being recruited. That was the chance you took when you hired someone overqualified; they might leave when they found something more in line with the picture they had for their future. She couldn't blame him for seizing the opportunities presented to him. Didn't she long to pursue the same goal? But she couldn't quit vet school to follow a yearling to Florida.

Dusk was falling, the fringes of long shadows softening before they disappeared entirely. But she wasn't ready to go inside yet, to resign herself to her books and the future they represented.

She dragged Twizzle from his babysitting duties, threw an exercise saddle on him because she'd sold his good saddle when she'd started vet school. He'd become too creaky to do much work, anyway. A hack once in a while was fine, though she'd been shamefully negligent in that department, opting instead for younger, sounder horses.

Twizzle was up for it, on his toes as soon as her seat hit the saddle — he'd always been spicy, and age had done nothing to dilute that. He made her forget the post-run chill she felt, her boots pulled unfashionably over the tights she'd worn to run. Racetrackers did not wear boots over their pants like English riders did — their boots went under jeans. So not cool, but when had she ever been cool? And what did it matter? There was no one out here to see her, anyway.

The perimeter of the hayfield was clear and while the second cut had come off, she didn't want to risk damaging the fragile alfalfa, so she kept to the margin. A neighbour had permission to ride out here, so there was a worn track, the footing relatively consistent. It wasn't the meticulously groomed racetrack surface she usually rode on these days, but it was safe.

She let Twizzle think he was running off with her, the wind rushing past her ears sweeping away the feelings. Just for a short stretch, because he wasn't fit, even though, ex-racehorse that he was, he might think otherwise. Better give him a bit of Bute tonight.

After a good curry and a brush, she returned him to his babysitting duties. Instead of going back to the house, she went to Geai's. Geai would know about the decision for Claire. He would console her, then chastise her and tell her to get over it.

His back was to her, settled in his favourite chair, the beer in his hand propped on the armrest; television on, volume low. Napoleon roused himself from a deep old-dog slumber, long black tail sweeping the air, and she crouched to greet him. Then the Lab waddled back to his person, resting his chin faithfully on Geai's knee. Geai automatically placed a hand on his head, scratching him behind one ear.

Liv was just about to ask Geai if he was feeling okay, her arrival not eliciting his customary greeting, when she caught sight of the old black and white wedding photo on the end table next to him. Then she remembered, and felt terrible for forgetting.

Four years today, it had been, since his wife Francie's death, rapidly consumed by a voracious cancer. As much as Liv knew losing his soulmate had torn him apart, he'd carried on stoically, only taking a week away from the farm to bury her at his hometown in the Laurentians. When he'd returned, he'd never left again, save for quick trips for groceries or the feed store. Maybe it was just as well he didn't let Liv shop for him; otherwise, he might never step off the farm at all.

She went to him, leaning over to give him a squeeze, Napoleon's tail thumping against the hardwood, though the black Lab didn't leave his post. There were no words she could say that would ever make up for his loss, so she took her usual spot on the end of his couch, drawing her knees to her chest, arms wrapped around them, and stared at the TV without caring what was on the screen.

Her own woes seemed trivial now. She would deal with them — learn how to stay in control of her reactions and emotions. The past couldn't dictate her life. She needed to devote her energy to more important things. Even without speaking, Geai gave her much-needed perspective. Claire was going, but she was alive and thriving, and Liv could look forward to seeing what the filly would become. She would visit Claire in Florida and New York. Claire would remember her. Horses — especially fillies — remembered everything.

She wouldn't give up. She'd find a way; transfer the dream Claire had represented to Sotisse's unborn foal. Count the days until the mare's due date in January. She had her own places to go; her own world to conquer. Now just wasn't the time.

CHAPTER TWENTY-THREE

EVEN EMILIE WAS silent this morning, the yearlings jogging three-abreast on the Triple Stripe training track. Arthur was in the middle and sometimes bumped the fillies on either side like he was looking for security, Emilie closest to the rail on Gemma, Liv on the outside with Claire.

The shy colt was coming along nicely. Nate had used the driving lines to get the colt used to the feeling of something moving on his sides, so he wouldn't totally freak out once it was Nate's legs there, and it had worked. He wouldn't go so far as to call the colt confident, but he was satisfied with Arthur's progress.

These warm, sunny days were numbered. Already there had been a couple of chilly nights and frosty mornings, the dip in temperature triggering colour changes in the leaves of the plentiful maples around the farm, dabs of yellow and red and orange brightening the landscape as the bossy greens gave up their hold.

In another month, the yearlings' introductory lessons would be complete and they'd get time off until the new year.

He'd be demoted to regular barn staff if he stuck around. *Not that you minded that, remember?* But... he had options. He could go to Florida himself, if he went for Trevor's offer.

Did he owe these people anything? Sure, he'd told Geai he planned to stick around, but no one in the horse business ever expected to be held to such things. Farm help came and went like barn cats. Loyalty and commitment were rare, and he'd only been here a month.

He wasn't afraid of winter — he had grown up in Alberta after all — but that didn't mean avoiding it wasn't appealing. That's what the elite did in this business, right? There wasn't a spot for him on the Triple Stripe team headed south this year. All he had was a spoken promise of a job at the track in the spring, and that six months was a lifetime. Trevor had promised he could be riding races by then, if not sooner, if he put his mind to it. This wasn't the only outfit in the province. But if he became a rider, bailing on these people would be something they wouldn't forget. He'd always be that guy. Then there was Arthur, still very much a work in progress... how could he leave the colt, not knowing if whoever finished the job would take the time to get it right? Liv and Emilie were both too busy to do it.

He could run off and try his luck with the big outfit — Faron's — or he could stay with the respected one and hope patience did indeed pay off.

They pulled up just past the gap and turned in. His colt stood between the two fillies, and Nate wondered if the little yearling felt as conspicuous as he did himself, between Liv and Emilie, his female bookends. Similar in appearance, polar in personality.

It was Liv who initiated the walk off, and Emilie who initiated the conversation.

"Are you coming to the races this aft, Nate?" she asked. "Just Stellar is running."

He knew that, of course. And it wasn't that the question was unexpected.

"No — sorry — I have somewhere else to be. I'll watch, though. Good luck." His eyes slid from Emilie to Liv, feeling like a traitor, even though his excuse was legitimate.

He deserved Liv's brows-raised half-smile in response to his wishy-washy answer. Why would he not just make it so, to be there for one of the farm's rising young stars making her stake debut? It was a late race; he could go to Will's after. He could make up for everything to everybody.

Arthur planted his front feet abruptly, hind end splaying beneath him, bringing Nate jarringly back to the here and now. Claire and Gemma arced in front as Liv and Emilie halted them, the fillies not as affronted by the pickup rolling to a stop a good fifty feet away. They formed an inadvertent protective barrier. Convinced he was safe, at least for the moment, the colt dropped his head, pressing his muzzle into Liv's leg for comfort.

"Sorry," Nate said, but didn't pull Arthur's head away.

Liv shrugged. "Whatever works."

Geai climbed slowly from the truck, speaking quietly as he approached. "Such a brave boy, hiding behind the girls."

The comment could have applied just as well to Nate as the colt. Not that he was hiding from Geai. Maybe he'd been avoiding him because he worried Geai would see through him. The old man saw stuff, in people and in horses.

Geai greeted Gemma first — she was clearly his favourite of the yearlings — then Claire. The colt lifted his muzzle and expelled a mild snort through nostrils open wide to take in the predator, his ears still locked forward.

"See, Arthur? Geai isn't scary," Emilie said.

He wasn't, not really, but Nate wondered if he could be.

Under all that congeniality, he figured the farm manager took no shit.

"I'll let you pass before I continue on my way," Geai said, not attempting to touch the colt, just allowing his presence to be felt; steady, non-threatening. "When you're done, will you come help me with the stallions, Nate? I could use a hand."

"Yeah, sure," he replied too quickly, a tremor in the pit of his stomach. When did Geai ever ask for help with the stallions? His gut was strongly suggesting it was about something else.

"Finally," Liv muttered. "He never lets anyone help. I've been telling him he needs to actually make his days off, days off."

"Careful, Nate," Emilie quipped, her lips twisting wryly. "You might make yourself indispensable around here."

He didn't think Emilie meant anything by that. She would have said something to him outright. It was Liv he could never read.

He found Geai in the stallion barn when he arrived. "Go get the big horse. Put it through his mouth and he'll be fine."

Nate knew exactly who he meant, and nodded, accepting with reverence the long leather stallion shank with a chain wrapped in Vetrap on one end and a big knot on the other. Despite his suspicions, he couldn't help feeling honoured he was being entrusted with the farm's most famous resident.

The "big horse" waited impatiently at the gate. Just Lucky wasn't big at all in stature, but he was in everything else: reputation, accomplishment, presence. It was a title bestowed upon a horse who commanded respect; a horse who had proven himself on the track and earned his position as the best in the barn.

The hardest part was getting the shank on without getting nipped by those quick teeth. The stallion might just be playing

— testing Nate to see what he could get away with — but if he connected, he'd leave a mark.

Just Lucky pranced beside him like he thought he was his great-great granddaddy Northern Dancer. Nate grinned but held the stallion with both hands on the shank, because that eye was all mischief, and it was trained on him.

"He must've been a handful on the track." Nate slipped out of the stall with all his digits intact.

"Ask Livvy," Geai said. "She galloped him a bit."

Of course she had. The information hit him with both admiration and jealousy.

"Can I get on him? This could be like some of those Kentucky farms where they exercise the stallions to keep them in shape for breeding season."

Geai didn't answer, his arms crossed, his gaze narrowing. *And here it comes.*

"I asked you when we started, if you intend to be around next year. Now I feel the need to ask if you'll be around next month."

He felt the old man's eyes when he refused to meet them, his own shifting with his feet. He didn't give an answer, because he didn't have one.

"If you can, some notice would be nice. It's not an easy time of year to find help. The best people go south." Disappointment wrapped in irony laced his tone as he relieved Nate of the loop of leather and chain. "You can go. I'll get Starway. I know you have someplace to be."

The dismissal stung, but it served him right.

He made it to Will's as promised, ready to catch up for a few hours before they went out. He'd showered off the horsiness and put on nice clothes, but didn't feel especially clean. Will didn't comment on his distraction; he actually didn't look particularly convinced Nate was even there to start with, not

177

that Nate could blame him. Gradually the music did its thing as they played some tunes, easing the tension. It felt just a bit like old times, back when they were teenagers in Calgary and joked about their band making it. Then the alarm he'd set on his phone went off to remind him to watch Just Stellar's race.

Will didn't complain, and even watched over his shoulder. The fillies were being loaded, filing into the starting gate one by one.

Just Stellar ran much like she had for her maiden win, sweeping up outside of horses on the turn for home and surging to match strides with the favoured leader. The two runners fought hard down the stretch, locked together until the Triple Stripe filly broke the showdown, inching ahead with each thrust of her head.

"Come on, Stella," he said, his tone more restrained than it would have been if he'd watched with the others at the track. A nose, then a head. At the wire she had a neck advantage.

He was happy for them. And sad for himself.

The camera view shifted to show the field galloping out, and his blood ran cold. Dave Johnson was pulling Stella up hard, the other fillies going around her.

"She's hurt," he said, his throat dry. He jammed his phone in his back pocket and grabbed his coat from the back of the couch, digging his keys out as he rushed for the door.

"What are you doing?" Will asked.

"I'm sorry, Will, really I am, but I have to go."

"Let me get this straight. You're blowing me off — again, and on my birthday, no less — for the place you're planning on leaving?"

"I'm not planning anything." He bit off the words, but his reaction was a revelation. Because why would these people care? They already questioned his commitment, so his appearance would be taken with a grain of salt. But it hit him he cared about those horses. Not that he hadn't cared about the ones he'd encountered at the Fort — his actions and reactions there had been things he couldn't get away from, and they made him think hard about the choices he'd be facing if he went that route. But he cared about those people too, even though he barely knew them, while he held no affection for the ones he'd met at the Faron outfit. The Triple Stripe crew had taken him in. Given him a place when he had no place.

"Can't you just call?" Will persisted.

Call? No. He needed to show up. "I'll meet you later. Promise."

There was no traffic on the 427 highway on the weekend, so it didn't take him long to get to Woodbine. He flashed his badge at the security gate, tapping the steering wheel while he waited for the sleepy guard to scan it before he was allowed into the backstretch.

The vet's black SUV was parked at the end of the barn, and he pulled up behind it. Jo was holding the filly on the shedrow while the vet positioned the x-ray machine, Liv decked out in the heavy blue lead apron and cumbersome leaded gloves as she held the plates in position by the filly's right fore. Roger stood to the side, observing.

None of them noticed him. He doubted he was even welcome here. But he waited, out of the way, watching.

Liv noticed him when she shouldered off the apron, surprise flashing in her eyes before she returned her attention to what the vet was saying to Jo and Roger. *Condylar fracture. Surgery.*

He jumped in with an offer to help carry out equipment. Liv slid him a sideways glance as she packed the apron away. He hadn't noticed till then she was wearing a sheath dress, a dusky blue that came close to matching her eyes, ballet flats on her feet. Go-racing clothes, not barn wear.

Jo already had bandages on Just Stellar, tied at the front of her stall with access to her haynet. The filly didn't seem in any distress. There was no dramatic rushing off to the clinic like the legendary filly she so reminded him of, Ruffian.

"When will they do the surgery?" he asked.

"Monday, probably," Liv said. "It's not an emergency. It would probably heal without it. It's just a minor fracture, non-displaced, but the internal fixation will ensure a better prognosis. They should be able to do it with a single lag screw to reconnect the condyle to the metacarpal." She fell easily into vet speak, finding a seat on a foot locker set against the outer rail, and he had enough anatomy knowledge left over from his aborted kinesiology program to translate. The condyle was the wedge-shaped bit fractured off the end of the cannon bone he'd caught a glimpse of in the images.

Nate wandered a few stalls down to the only other face he recognized, Paz. The old gelding looked hopeful, stretching his neck over the stall yoke, but Nate's pockets were empty. "What is he today? Pony or racehorse?"

"Pony," Liv said. "He wasn't himself galloping this morning. Came back with a bit of heat in his tendon. We ultrasounded it and there's no tear, just inflammation, but he's done."

What a day, but it could have been so much worse. Both horses would be fine.

He should probably get back to Will's, but he lingered. It wasn't about the girl — this strange, quiet girl. He'd made that mistake before, changing direction to be the man he thought he needed to be for someone else, and he'd still lost out. He was here for the horses, because they'd never let him down. And this barn, this girl... they were on the same page. The horses came first.

"I'd better go," he finally said, standing just out of Paz's reach. "On my way to my friend's birthday party."

"Thanks for checking in." Liv met his eyes with what looked like respect he didn't deserve and a question he needed to answer.

CHAPTER TWENTY-FOUR

STELLA'S INJURY wasn't life-threatening, though Liv supposed any time a horse sustained a fracture it could end up that way. The orthopedic surgeon invited her to observe; she accepted the front-row seat.

Everything about the injury made the filly a candidate for a standing procedure done with sedation and a nerve block of the leg instead of lying her on the table under a general anesthetic. It reduced the risk of complications so much because recovery from general anesthetic always had the potential to go sideways with horses. With the filly sedated, leg clipped and scrubbed, the surgeon poised with the scalpel, ready to start the incision. She wished it were in her hand. Then it came to her, a glimmer of enlightenment. This could be the answer.

She didn't need to be a track vet. She didn't need to be the farm vet. She could be a surgeon; put horses back together instead of being party to tearing them apart. All her reticence disappeared as she watched — asking questions, peering at the in-operation radiographs, itching to be the one with the knife and power tools. It must've impressed the surgeon, because after he finished, he suggested they talk about her doing a surgical internship once she'd graduated.

She didn't leave until Just Stellar was bandaged, back in the stall at the clinic, and the sedation had worn off. It was late enough she had a legitimate excuse to skip her ride on Claire. Not that she wanted excuses; she wanted to be with the filly as much as she could before Claire left with the Florida horses. But tonight, a hello and a few peppermints — now that she knew the filly liked them — and maybe she'd try to get to bed early for a change.

Pulling up to the training barn, lights already illuminated the aisle. She heard singing first, then as she peeked in the end of the barn, found Arthur in the first stall on the left, Nate currying away. What was that song?

Arthur noticed her first, Nate cutting his tune short when he caught up with the colt. "Hey. How'd the surgery go?"

"Good," she said simply. "He looks like he's trying to enjoy being inside."

"It's never going to be his favourite place, but he's coping."

Maybe she should try singing, too. It was just a different kind of breathing, wasn't it?

He slipped the halter over the colt's ears and left the stall, dropping the grooming tools in the tote by the door. Liv wandered a few stalls down to Claire.

"I left her in for you, just in case," Nate said.

"Thanks," she said. "She's due a day off."

He paused on his way to the tack room, watching as she pulled a mint from her pocket and offered it to Claire.

"She's a nice filly," he said.

He didn't mean that she was pretty, or sweet, even if she was all that. He meant she was classy. He meant she might have talent. She might have that something that would make her a racehorse.

"I hope so," Liv said. Even if it wasn't her that got to develop the filly from here, she wanted for Claire what she couldn't have herself.

She turned to face him, still close enough she could feel the filly's breath on her neck. "The yearlings will be done in a couple of weeks. I know you haven't given notice, but I don't like to assume. I realize you have other opportunities."

He rocked his weight onto one leg, meeting her eyes, but didn't respond.

"There are few secrets on the backstretch," she said wryly, her lips crimping on one side before she pressed them together. "I wouldn't blame you for going. If I could go to Florida for the winter, I would. Are you staying?"

He didn't speak, and she felt as if she was holding her breath. Claire nudged her, like she was reminding Liv to inhale. She admitted she'd miss him — or the idea of him — if he left.

"I'd like to finish what I've started."

She nodded, surprised by the relief that washed over her. "Good. You fit, Miller."

For a split second, she felt they were a perfect match, because they would never be. He would eventually go his own way — on to ride — and she would go hers. They would travel divergent paths. And part of her was sad about that; a very small part. A part of her lost long ago. But it passed.

"I don't know why anyone would want to go to Florida anyway," he said.

Liv grinned. "I agree. The spiders are massive. And the fire ants could kill you."

"Not to mention gators that eat small dogs."

"And children."

"I'm told there are wild boar at Payson Park. Rumour, or fact?" he asked.

"It could be true."

"Not to mention spending afternoons on the beach burning our pale Canadian hides," he added.

"Boring," she agreed.

"And going to the races at Gulfstream."

"Then there's Wellington. So pretentious." She rolled her eyes.

"I hear polo's a drag too."

She turned back to the filly at her shoulder, her smile fading. "Claire's going."

His expression sobered. "I'm sorry. Next year."

She caught his smile, his wistful eyes, and returned them. "Next year."

Nate went back to the apartment — his apartment. He had work to do. It would take time to build Geai's trust, prove his loyalty, develop the belief that he'd stay. Liv, though? That was beyond him. He thought he saw some of himself reflected in her; a distant dream, a taste of something he wanted but couldn't quite have. It was hard to put a finger on it.

He didn't know her well enough to speculate what was under her wall. On the surface, she seemed straightforward. It was simple: she liked horses better than people. She liked her privacy. He could respect that, even relate to it. They might just be kindred spirits. A ghost of a good thing. That made him smile.

With the whole Fort Erie fiasco — that was how he'd always think of that morning — he'd fallen victim to the fear of missing out. Did he want to ride? Sure. In time. It was that patience thing again. Good things come to those who wait. He still felt he had too much stuff to fix. He had to do it right. He'd messed up enough.

He turned on the lamp resting on top of the piano, its light bathing the keys he'd so far left untouched. That photo of him, and her, and his brothers was safely in the shadow.

The bench was hard, but his fingers ached to play. He stretched them over the white and black pattern hovering for a moment like he'd done every time he'd tried sitting here, but this time they connected, and the notes came, building to a melody, the music making it clear he was exactly where he needed to be.

---

*If you enjoyed **Bright, Broken Things**, please take a moment to review it! BookBub and Amazon reviews are most helpful, but sharing of any kind is wonderful. Thank you!*

THE END

A NOTE TO THE READER

First of all, thank you for reading this prequel to the Good Things Come series. The first chapter of Book One, **Good Things Come,** follows, jumping in with the impending birth of Sotisse's much-anticipated foal!

Get it in paperback, ebook or audio

Get the box set of books 1-3

Get the box set of books 1-5

If you would consider taking a moment to leave a review for **Bright, Broken Things** on BookBub or your favourite retailer, especially if you received a free copy, I'd be so grateful. Reviews help bring other readers to the series and inspire authors to write more of the books you love. I always love to hear from readers, too. You can email me anytime at linda@lindashantz.com

A side note on this book: I freely admit I took some liberties with the timing of the third-year curriculum at the Ontario Veterinary College for artistic purposes. If you're a recent or present vet student there, please don't hate me!

Thank you so much again for reading. Now, get tied on for the rest of the series, because it's going to be a wild ride!

"Glee," a pencil drawing © Linda Shantz

GOOD THINGS COME BOOK ONE:
CHAPTER ONE

THERE WAS a weight to the stillness, the tangerine band streaking across the inky horizon holding something contrary to the promise of a new day. Liv's nostrils stuck together as she drew in a breath. *So cold.* Maybe not as cold as the winters she remembered as a child *à Montréal,* but the record-breaking polar vortex sweeping Southern Ontario made her forget some of her hardy *Québécois* pride. She tugged her hood down and pushed gloved hands deeper into the pockets of her down-filled jacket, the squeak of her boots on the laneway's hard-packed snow like Styrofoam to her ears.

She'd take these frigid mornings over what was to come. Inventing creative ways to keep her fingers from freezing as she legged up feisty two-year-olds in the indoor arena was still preferable to hours spent imprisoned in the University of Guelph's stuffy lecture halls and labs. Just three more days of winter break, and that's what she'd be back to—pursuing a degree she wasn't convinced she wanted.

Back to reality. Back to expectations.

Light spilled from the barn's overhead apartment, and she

almost expected to feel warmth as she sliced through the bright pool of light in her path. She slid through the side door, frost condensing on her eyelashes, her face starting to thaw, and a chorus of whinnies greeting her even before she switched on the lights.

"'Morning girls," she called, inspiring another singsong as she ducked into the feed room and scooped the breakfast ration of grain into a pail. When she turned the corner to the well-lit aisle, the faces of two mares jutted out of boxes on either side. The third, though...

"Hey, 'Tisse, what's up?"

Sotisse stood in the corner of the deeply bedded straw, oblivious. The mare took a deliberate turn, huge belly swollen with the life she carried; her tail slightly raised, patches of sweat on her flank and neck darkening her bright chestnut coat to liver. Liv's heart rate took off, and she scrambled to feed the other two horses.

Nerves and muscles were at odds with her brain, but she summoned enough self-control to keep from racing back to the feed room, the grain bucket clattering to the ground. Vapour from the hot water flushed her face as she filled a stainless steel pail. In her other hand she scooped up the foaling kit she'd prepared—just in case—and power-walked back to the stall.

Hold it together, Liv. Her hands were trembling so badly she fumbled with the elastic bandage as she wrapped Sotisse's long golden tail, something she should be able to do in her sleep.

Three weeks. Sotisse was three weeks early. Not technically premature, but still.

She glanced at the time on her phone, then up at the ceiling. Both she and the exercise rider who lived upstairs were due at the training barn for seven, but she definitely wasn't going to make it now. Calling on an extra set of hands was the sensible thing to do, even though complications were rare. This was Sotisse, Papa's favourite racemare, having her first foal, by none other than Just Lucky. And she could be as practical as she wanted about the breeding business, but there was no denying she'd been waiting for this foal. This foal was special.

Foaling was messy, and fast. But there was something intimate about it too, ushering a newborn into this world, and part of her didn't want to share it with a stranger. Because even though Nate Miller had been working on the farm since September, he was really still a stranger to her.

She'd just get him to hold Sotisse while she checked the foal's position and washed under her tail and udder. Once she knew all was well, he could go. Taking two steps at a time, she flew up the stairwell.

Meaning to knock softly, she rapped a staccato beat on the apartment door. There was no hiding the welling combination of panic and excitement in her eyes. The whole being professional and under control thing was definitely not coming off at the moment. She was ready to knock again when the door swung open.

"Everything okay?" Nate stepped back to let her inside, eyebrow tweaked, but she stayed where she was, and dodged his eyes when they landed on hers.

Damn the way her stomach tumbled. Normal, physiological response, right? Sure he was good-looking, but she had enough trouble being taken seriously because she looked fourteen without acting it. She'd leave the gushing to her younger sister Emilie, and the girls who worked on the farm—all of whom had applauded her for hiring him to break yearlings last summer. She'd given him the job because of his experience and references, not because a hot guy would be a welcome addition to the female-dominated staff.

"Sotisse is in labour. I need someone to hold her while I

check the foal's position. I won't keep you long." Words ran together, the heat wafting from the apartment threatening to turn her into a puddle of sweat. *Winter? What winter?*

"She's pretty early, isn't she?"

Liv nodded, already dashing back down the stairs.

Sotisse was sinking to her knees in the straw, glancing uncomfortably at her side before rocking back to roll as she tried to adjust the uncomfortable pressure inside her. The mare righted herself, resting, her well-sprung rib cage heaving with laboured breaths before she pitched into another roll, hooves clattering against the wall's wooden boards. She lurched back to her feet, circling with head low, steam rising.

Liv discarded her coat and adjusted her dark ponytail before sliding on a sterile sleeve, aware of Nate's appearance beside her. She waited, balanced on the balls of her feet, shaking her arms loose at her sides like a runner ready to step into the starting block.

"No..."

The word caught in her throat; the sac appearing under the mare's bandaged tail gleaming red instead of pearly white. Nate was already dragging open the door, like he must know what this meant. *Red bag delivery, placenta previa, premature detachment of the placenta*...more importantly, the foal wasn't getting oxygen.

Liv grabbed the sharp scissors from the foaling kit, Nate already at Sotisse's head. She sliced through the thick membrane, a pungent soup of blood, faeces and amniotic fluid sluicing out, soaking her through jeans and long johns and coursing down the mare's hocks. Reaching inside the birth canal to find the foal, her chest seized—one tiny foot was missing from the expected triad of two hooves and a nose.

"You need to get this going," Nate said, his eyes locking onto hers.

"I know that," she snapped, stepping back and ripping off the sleeve. "There's a leg caught."

She peeled off layers until she was stripped to a tank top, beyond any memory of cold, and drew on a fresh sleeve. Sotisse's contractions were powerful, closing in on her arm as she eased it inside the mare, following the foal's neck past the pelvic rim to the shoulder wedged against it. How could such a tiny baby get it so wrong? Not that it wasn't a good thing the foal was small, because it might be what made the difference between getting it out alive instead of dead. Braced against the mare's hindquarters, she pushed the shoulder back and found the uncooperative limb, stretching farther to cup the soft hoof in her hand, struggling to flip it up to join its mate. *Got it.*

Liv withdrew her arm and stepped back, still humming with adrenaline. Now they needed to get it out. Fast. "Turn her loose."

Sotisse lumbered around the stall, sweat and straw matting her thick coat, then buckled into the bedding and flattened herself with a grunt. Liv dropped to her knees, Nate right with her, the foal's tiny feet inching out with every contraction. They each grasped a leg, and Liv looked at him sideways. Nate nodded, and when the next contraction came, they pulled.

"C'mon, 'Tisse." Liv tried not to give in to the desperation creeping into her voice.

"You got this, momma," Nate murmured. "Just one more push to get those shoulders clear and we'll do the rest, promise."

He sounded a lot calmer than Liv felt. They strained with the mare, Liv clenching her jaw and putting her bodyweight behind one last heroic heave, and the foal's shoulders popped through. Another grunt from all three of them, and Nate and Liv drew the foal out onto the straw with a slippery mess of blood and membrane and fluid. Liv fretfully looked for signs of life.

Nate reached for the towels, passing her one, and started to vigorously rub the small, still, body. Liv lifted the foal's head, propping its shoulder against her own hip as she cupped the tiny muzzle to clear the nostrils.

"Filly," Nate said with a quick peek under the wispy tail.

"She's not breathing," Liv responded flatly, overwhelming dread paralyzing her as she cradled the foal's head in her lap.

"Get out of the way."

She was too dumbfounded to protest as he double-checked the foal's airway, stretched out the neck, then closed off the far nostril to start resuscitation. The foal's delicate rib cage rose and fell with the timing of his breaths, and as much as it irked Liv that she wasn't the one doing it, it made no sense to interrupt him. She crept closer to check the filly's pulse, and noticed Nate had stopped, his lips moving soundlessly, eyes fixed on the filly's side. They both saw the faint flutter.

"You got her." Liv pressed her eyes shut, opening them again to assure herself it hadn't been her imagination.

"Welcome to the planet, baby girl," Nate said softly.

Neither of them moved, watching as each breath came more strongly than the last. Sotisse stirred with a low rumble, rocking up onto her sternum and curling her neck towards the foal. Liv turned to Nate, at a loss as to how to express the emotions flooding her, so she pushed herself to her feet instead.

She grabbed the door frame as her legs cramped, then reached down for a dry towel and tossed it to him. "Stay with her?"

Her legs slowly regained function as she shuffled to the office, heartbeat tempering. The newborn foal's heritage surrounded her on the walls of the small room—framed images of their stallion, Just Lucky, winning the Queen's Plate, and Sotisse's victory in the Canadian Oaks. A large oil painting of the pair posing on either side of farm manager Geai Doucet

dominated the room from behind a huge old desk. Liv paused—
she could never just ignore that painting—then picked up the
landline, not trusting the reception of her cell phone, and put in
a call to Geai, leaving a message.

By the time Liv returned, the foal was alert, her long
forelegs stretched in front of her. Nate still rubbed the baby
with the towel, a huge grin on his face as the filly shook her
head and struck out with a hoof, trying to get her hind end
underneath her. Sotisse was on her feet, supervising anxiously
over his shoulder. While it got old, the way Emilie and the girls
went on about Nate—the charm, the sandy blond hair, the
azure eyes—he looked pretty good at the moment.

A rush of incoming air from the door interrupted the sentiment, Liv glancing up the aisle. A fresh smile took over her face
as Geai appeared around the corner. "You must not have been
far away."

The old man ambled towards her and threw a well-bundled
arm around her shoulders, pulling her into him as he squeezed.
"Put some clothes on! It's freezing!"

"I'd forgotten," Liv said wryly, bending down to scoop up
the discarded pile. She eased her shirt on, everything aching.

Geai peered through the stall door. "A filly?"

Nate nodded and draped the towel over his shoulder as he
climbed stiffly to his feet, hand outstretched. Geai grasped it
firmly.

"All good?" The farm manager turned back to Liv.

"I could have done without the drama, and some oxygen
would have been nice...but yeah, now, so far." The list of things
that could still go wrong lurked in her brain.

Geai crossed his arms, the corners of his eyes crinkling as
they went from Liv to Nate. "Great work, you two. But who's
getting on the horses this morning while our two exercise riders
are here playing midwife?"

Nate glanced at Liv with a smirk. "I'll get going. Don't expect I'll see you over there anytime soon."

"I think you're on your own this morning, sorry." Her sweater hid the upward curve of her lips as she pulled it over her head, the adrenaline wearing off and leaving her with a chill. "Thank you," she said, which was totally inadequate, but she wasn't good at putting feelings into words.

He flashed an easy grin, zipping his jacket and extracting a toque from the pocket. "Pleasure was all mine."

Maybe it was a good thing she was going back to school, because that, there, was a distraction, and there was no room for distraction in any of her plans.

"At least her early arrival means you'll get a few days to dote on her before your classes start, eh?" Geai's voice pulled her back to the filly in the stall.

She wasn't going to think about classes right now. She fished a tiny cup out of the foaling kit and filled it with chlorhexidine, then went back in, interrupting Sotisse's devoted cleaning of her new daughter to douse the foal's umbilical stump. Sotisse rumbled worriedly, bumping Liv with her nose.

"Don't worry, momma, I'll just be a second."

The filly kicked and struggled, amazing Liv with her rally. There were no markings on the jumble of legs, and only a few white hairs on her small wedge of a head, bobbing as her mother resumed her doting. A defiant whinny escaped from the filly's throat.

"Those lungs seem to be working fine now." Liv grinned at Geai.

"*On dirait une p'tite chique,*" Geai said, lapsing back into French now that Nate was gone.

Chique—that name was going to stick. The comparison was amusing, but fitting—the filly kind of looked like a little quid of tobacco someone had chewed up and spit out on the straw. Liv went in once more to give the foal an enema, and started removing the soiled bedding, replacing it with a deep, dry, bed, banked up the walls.

Geai's steady gaze landed on her when she rejoined him. "You will make a great vet. But I'm not sure you can practice veterinary medicine and be ready to ride this one in the Plate in three and a half years."

"They're all Plate horses at this stage," Liv scoffed, deflecting the way he pinpointed her real dream with logic. Because that was the dream—to ride races, the Plate the ultimate goal, this filly worthy of a place in her fantasy. She'd made it this far, overcoming her first hurdle and moving on to the next, all legginess and hope.

Geai chuckled and pushed up the sleeve of his heavy coat to check his watch. "I'll leave you to it. Keep me posted." He gave Liv a pat on the back and ambled off.

She tossed Sotisse a flake of hay and shrugged into her coat, hugging it around herself as she headed to the feed room to make the mare a hot mash. Then she left mare and foal to bond, and in the warmth of the office collapsed into the chair behind the desk to write up the foaling report, the painting of Lucky and Sotisse overseeing.

The Queen's Plate—Canada's most prestigious race, restricted to three-year-old Thoroughbreds foaled north of the forty-ninth parallel. Twelve hundred foals might be born across this country that spring; a hundred might be nominated for the classic; as many as twenty might go postward. Only one would get their picture taken in the winner's circle under the royal purple and gold blanket of flowers. One winning team would be on the podium accepting the fifty gold sovereigns from the Queen's representative. *Many are called, few are chosen*...and only one comes home first.

Liv wrote it down like a prophecy: SOTISSE: *January 2, 7:05AM, dk.b./br.filly by Just Lucky...*

Breed the best to the best, they said. And hope for the best.

Her own future was as mapped out as Chique's. She'd gone along with the assumption she'd become a vet for so long; now here she was, with a year and a half left of the DVM program and a surgical internship hers for the taking after she graduated, questioning the whole thing. Sure, it would be an asset to have a vet in the family, between the farm, and the string of racehorses at the track, currently wintering in Florida. Liv's heart was with those horses, her passion pitch perfect on their backs, not at the end of a scalpel or reading radiographs. There was no doing both, because both were all-or-nothing paths.

She finished up the foaling report and went back to the stall. The little filly struggled with determination to get to her feet.

"Let's see if I can help you out."

Positioning herself behind the foal's rump, she wrapped her fingers around the base of Chique's tail, and when the filly's next scrambling effort came, Liv scooped an arm under the narrow ribcage for added support. The filly bobbled, but with Liv steadying her, parked a leg at each corner. Chique gave a definitive snort and minced forward, instinctively looking for her first meal.

"You're a fighter, *ti-Chique.*"

Being a vet was a responsible choice. A safe choice. Giving up what she'd spent years in school for? Was crazy. Period. But Liv had done sensible her whole life. Maybe this filly was her chance to break free.

Look for Good Things Come in print, audio and ebook at your favourite retailer!

ACKNOWLEDGMENTS

Once again I'm grateful to my beta readers, who take time out of their own busy schedules to provide invaluable help. They keep me on track with details and readability and help catch stray typos (though some inevitably make it through, so if you see one, don't be shy about emailing me). Thank you, Allison Litfin, Bev Harvey, Nathalie Drolet and Kristen Frederick DVM (who also makes sure my veterinary details are right).

Thank you and welcome to my new early readers, June Monteleone, Elise Cooper, Ariana Feldberg, Sharrell Kline, Mary Hathaway and Erika Keller Thomas and Claire (not to be confused with Claire the horse, though she is a fan!) Burnham.

And a nostalgic nod to the horse people I have worked with in my life. I've been blessed to have worked with the best!

ABOUT THE AUTHOR

It was an eight-year-old me, frustrated that all the horse racing novels I read were about the Derby, not the Plate, who first put pencil to three-ring paper and started what would become this story. Needless to say, we've both grown up a bit since then.

I began working at the track before I finished high school, and after graduating the following January, took a hotwalking job at Payson Park in Florida. Once back at Woodbine, I started grooming and galloping. While the backstretch is exciting, I found I was more at home on the farm — prepping and breaking yearlings, nightwatching and foaling mares. Eventually I started my own small layup/broodmare facility, and in the last few years I've transitioned into retraining and rehoming. Somewhere along the way I did go back to school and get a degree. I should probably dust it off and frame it one day.

I live on a small farm in Ontario, Canada, with my off-track Thoroughbreds and a young Border Collie, and I'm probably better known for painting horses than writing about them — if you like my covers, check out my artwork at www.lindashantz.com

Author Photo courtesy of Ellen Schoeman Photography

Made in the USA
Columbia, SC
19 January 2023

10707597R00115